**"I'm not going** _____
**I wasn't smart e** _____
**business."**

Having said that, Fleming couldn't help weighing Jason up as the villain of her bad holiday season.

As they walked into the hotel, Lyle Benjamin appeared at the top of the cellar stairs, his arms full of firewood.

"Not you, too, Fleming?" he asked, glancing from Jason to her.

She blushed.

"The gossip in this town defeats any need for the internet," Jason said impatiently.

"Sorry." Lyle sent Fleming an apologetic look. He carried the wood to the hearth near his check-in counter and tossed a log into the fire. "Table for two?"

"No." Fleming flinched as Jason's voice echoed her own.

"I'll call down for room service," the banker said.

Fleming breathed a sigh of relief. She had to create a battle plan. This man wanted his bank in the black. He might say he was helping her, but he'd take the Mainly Merry Christmas shop if shutting her down bettered his bottom line.

Dear Reader,

It's holiday time in Bliss, Tennessee! Jason Macland's in Bliss to rescue his family's bank. Unfortunately, that means he might have to foreclose on some bad loans, including the one for Mainly Merry Christmas, a shop run by Fleming Harris.

Fleming believes in the spirit of the holidays. Jason just wants to do his job and move on to the next one. Determined to remain detached from the citizens in the hometown he doesn't even remember, every day for him is like a visit from some ghost of his past. Will he learn about joy from Fleming? And will he help her finally believe that a loving, honorable man can stay?

I'm so happy to be back in Bliss, the Smoky Mountain town where *Now She's Back* and *Owen's Best Intentions* are also set. As always, my visit back was like a trip through memories of my own childhood in the Smokies. I hope you'll find your own sweet memories bounding up out of this story of celebrating love.

All the best,

*Anna Adams*

# HEARTWARMING

## *A Christmas Miracle*

——

USA TODAY Bestselling Author

*Anna Adams*

**HARLEQUIN®** HEARTWARMING™

Recycling programs
for this product may
not exist in your area.

ISBN-13: 978-0-373-36814-3

A Christmas Miracle

Printed in U.S.A.

**Anna Adams** wrote her first romance on the beach in wet sand with a stick. These days she uses pens, software or napkins and a crayon to write the kinds of stories she loves best—romance that involves everyone in the family and often the whole community. Love, like a stone tossed into a lake, causes ripples to spread and contract, bringing conflict and well-meaning "help" from the people who care most.

Visit the Author Profile page
at Harlequin.com for more titles.

For Pete, and for all of us who love you. My memories of you will always bristle with joy and your laugh. I miss you so much, but you are not lost to any of us.

# CHAPTER ONE

DESPITE BEING GOOD friends with technology, Fleming Harris answered Jason Macland's summons to the bank with printed copies of all the paperwork she could find. She knew very little about Jason. He was the son of the bank's owner, but he was a stranger to the remote Smoky Mountains town of Bliss, Tennessee, not having set foot there in decades.

Fleming had heard stories. People said Jason was his father's hired gun, brought in to close accounts, trim fat, sew up loopholes.

She swallowed a lump of panic as she smoothed her skirt beneath the pile of folders on her lap. Across the room, Hilda Grant, Jason's admin, shared an empathetic smile that worried Fleming.

Her shop, Mainly Merry Christmas, was her future and her past. She'd grown up "working" with her single mother behind the counter, playing with the wooden trains that doubled as decoration during the holiday season, learning to count by handing out change. Her pride was tied up in the twinkling lights and the beautiful ornaments.

And the burdensome loan payments. She'd missed only two. Shame burned her. *Only.*

This bank guy wouldn't have summoned her if he wasn't about to threaten her shop.

"You can go in now," Hilda said.

At the same time, the office door opened and a man emerged, lean and tall, with wary dark eyes and dark brown hair. His gaze caught her as if she were in a spotlight.

"Hello," she said, when what she meant was *What do you want from me?*

"Please, Ms. Harris." He held the door for her, ushering her inside. His mouth, a generous slash of masculine fullness, did not curve.

She stood, and her legs felt as stiff as planks as she passed in front of him, into the office of the bank's president, William Gaines. Some said Mr. Gaines had taken a pre-Thanksgiving vacation, but she'd also heard he'd been fired.

"Mr. Macland," she began, keeping things on a formal footing.

"Jason." He shut the door behind her and

gestured with an open, capable hand toward the leather couch in front of a wide fireplace, where a tablet was set up on a rustic, scarred coffee table. "Let's not pretend you don't know why I've asked you here," he said.

Her mouth opened in surprise at his abruptness. She shut it. She wouldn't give up the store to some bully. She'd find a way to fight him.

He waited for her to sit. "Would you like coffee?"

"I'd like to get this over with." She tried to appear more confident than she felt. "I know I'm behind on payments."

His hard mouth softened. He sat in the chair kitty-corner to the sofa and turned the tablet so they could both view the screen. "That's exactly what I want to discuss." He straightened one leg, looking more like a jock than the loan police. Muscles and strength. Power, leashed by frustration. The observation unsettled her even more.

He continued. "Mr. Paige, the former loan officer—"

"Former?" Bliss's ultra-busy grapevine had fallen down on reporting part of the news cycle.

Untroubled by her interruption, Jason merely breathed in and went on, his husky voice claiming all her attention. "Mr. Paige was let go because he approved loans for certain of his clients under terms that were inappropriate."

"I'm not understanding you." She stood. "Are you suggesting I've done something wrong?"

He glanced down at the sofa, clearly asking her to sit again. "Not at all. You are behind on your loan, but that's not why I've asked you here. Mr. Paige was skimming from several of the accounts and I believe he knew you'd never be able to continue to repay under the terms he offered you. I assume he meant to run before my father caught on to what's been happening here."

"The bank did something wrong?" A moment's relief made Fleming realize she hadn't breathed freely for two months. Was there a way out of this mess she seemed to be making of her life? "Am I going to keep the store?"

His expression didn't change. She had the feeling he'd been repeating this conversation with other clients like her.

"I'm offering you a chance to secure a new

loan with more affordable terms," he explained. "Mr. Paige will be speaking to the district attorney. The bank is making restitution for his actions."

"So that's your point." She followed his blunt lead. "I'm not interested in suing the bank. I only care about keeping my store, and I thought you were going to tell me I'm about to lose it."

He nodded, reaching for the tablet. His hands distracted her again as he slid his fingers across the screen, his glance lifting to her face.

This man held her future in his spreadsheets. Fleming had some dreams she wanted to make reality, and keeping Mainly Merry Christmas for her own children was one of them.

"Not everyone has reacted as calmly as you have," he said.

"You're trying to measure whether I'm aware of what's happening?"

He sat back. "No, Ms. Harris. I don't doubt your intelligence."

"Fleming."

His smile caught her unawares.

She didn't want to be attracted to him.

"Fleming," he said, and turned back to the tablet. "If you're agreeable, we'll start from the beginning with a loan for you. I don't usually work in the loan office, but since this is my family's bank, I have the same concern you do that we all succeed in Bliss."

"Are you saying I have recourse? Have I overpaid?"

A commotion interrupted from the outer office. Raised voices and thudding as if something had dropped on the floor.

Before Jason could speak, the door burst open. A tall glass vase tumbled and broke and furniture skidded as a man dived over the back of the couch, trying to plant his fist in Jason's face.

With barely any effort at all, Jason stood and twisted out of the intruder's reach. Jason climbed over the table and put himself between Fleming and his attacker, who'd ended up on the floor.

"Paige," Jason said, as he pulled Fleming up and tucked her behind his back. The man at their feet scrambled for handholds on the table and the sofa.

Without thinking, Fleming flattened her

hands on Jason's back. "We need the police," she gasped.

He urged her toward the office door. "Get out of here."

She froze. "I can't just leave you with him." Walk away and leave someone else in possible danger? She looked into his eyes, and in that moment of ugly violence a bond formed between them. She took a step back, but not because she was afraid of the intruder.

"Stay there," another voice barked.

Two armed, uniformed guards bounded over the furniture to scoop up the bank's former loan officer. One hustled their prey, stunned by his fall, out of the room. The other, a long-time acquaintance of Fleming's, faced Jason.

"We've called the police. They're on their way."

"Did he hurt anyone out there?" Jason glanced toward the reception area.

"No, sir. Seemed intent on getting in here. Fleming, are you okay? Are you hurt?"

"I'm fine, Mr. Oakes." With relief flowing to every extremity, but feeling incredibly awkward at the same time, she hid her face as she bent to gather the files she'd dumped on the faded, flowery rug. "He must have tripped on these when he landed."

"Let me help you." Jason's hand brushed hers as she picked up a file, which she dropped immediately.

Mr. Oakes, who'd also provided security for high school football games in years past, managed to retrieve the rest and handed the pile to her. "You should go home."

"I have to go to work." She stared into the hall, where Paige suddenly reappeared, writhing against his captor's hold. "He never said a word."

"He made his point, though." Jason looked calm, but his voice seemed a thread huskier. This time, as she stared, fascinated, he looked away, feeling for his tablet underneath the chair. "You might want to stay in case the police…"

"Oh. Okay."

"I'll email you the information I was hoping to discuss. We can talk about it again."

After seeing him attacked, the last thing she wanted to talk about was her money troubles. It was embarrassing. If she lost the shop, she'd lose her home. She'd lose her mother's respect. She'd lose her own.

"I trusted Mr. Paige." How on earth could she believe that Jason Macland, whose family name was on the bank, really wanted to help her out of a financial catastrophe?

"A lot of people did," Jason said, "including my father."

So he wasn't here just to fix the bank. He also had someone he didn't want to disappoint.

"MR. MACLAND, that was your last appointment." Hilda was already buttoning her coat. "If you don't mind, I'd like to go home."

By the time the police had left, Jason and Hilda and Fleming Harris had formed a triad—the first people Paige had found the guts to attack in person, rather than hiding behind a predatory loan. "You're coming back tomorrow?" Jason asked.

She nodded. "As long as that man's in the county jail."

Which was apparently over the ridge that almost completely surrounded the town.

"You don't happen to have Ms. Harris's phone number?" he asked. Fleming had lingered at the edges of Jason's mind since she'd left the office. She wasn't the only person

Paige had cheated. There was the man whose house was in danger of foreclosure, the two elderly ladies who'd retired to Bliss to open an ice cream parlor. Others, too. And all the while, Jason kept thinking of the woman who'd refused to leave a man she didn't know when he might be in danger.

"I'll find the number for you." Hilda opened a file on her computer and then wrote the phone number on a slip of paper. "She must have been afraid."

As Paige had sailed past Fleming's shoulder, every story of workplace violence he'd ever heard had replayed in Jason's head. His only thought had been to protect her, the innocent bystander who happened to be in his office at the worst possible time.

"I thought I'd offer to meet her somewhere else," he said.

"That's kind."

Jason managed not to laugh. *Kind* was not a word often used to describe him.

He'd had to make hard decisions before. He normally analyzed a failing business, provided structures and policies for dragging it back into financial profit and then moved on to the next troubled company. He'd never had the slightest urge to work for his father in any of the Macland banks. His involvement now was supposed to be a favor for his grandfather, who'd actually been the one to notice something was going on in Bliss. Jason meant to be in and out, with his report sewn up by the first week in January.

He took the piece of paper. "Thanks, Hilda, and listen, you don't have to be afraid," he said. "The guy's angry with me because I'm the one who told him he got caught."

"I'm sure a few days in a cell will make him a lot happier."

"We can hope he's also cheated any attorney who's capable of getting him bail. If you hear him coming down that hall again, jump in the nearest closet."

"I've already made that plan." She turned back to her screen. "You might try meeting Fleming at her shop. My girls and I spend a lot of time there this time of year. The Harrises put on activities for children, and Fleming's mother makes the best hot cocoa I've ever tasted."

He pushed the phone number into his pocket. "That's a good idea. I'm curious about a place that sells holiday ornaments all year long."

Or maybe he was curious about the owner of such a place. The year held other holidays. A smart business owner would consider diversifying. Fleming might be able to use his expertise.

FLEMING MANNED HER post behind the counter until the last of the pedestrians walking past on the sidewalk had disappeared for the day. The night before Thanksgiving was never busy, but she felt anxious. Bliss had never felt anything but safe until today.

Maybe a few customers would have taken her mind off this morning. Business would pick up on Friday.

Her stomach growled. She'd been so intent on making the store as inviting as her mother had when Fleming was a child that she'd forgotten to eat. The hotel at the end of the courthouse square had been doing a turkey dinner with fixings all week.

If she went to the hotel tonight, she'd probably have leftovers for a sandwich tomorrow, and she could finish making the shop shine by Friday morning.

Fresh eyes, she told herself.

It certainly wasn't that she felt reluctant to go home alone.

She put on her coat and shoved the warm gloves she'd worn in this morning's heavy frost into her pockets. She left Christmas lights twinkling in the windows and around the long wooden counter and set the shop's alarm, then locked up before heading for the hotel.

Outside, the streets were almost empty. Earlier in the week, garlands had begun to go up, but the decorations weren't yet complete. What with the danger of losing the shop and that Paige guy's rage this morning, she finally admitted her world felt off balance tonight.

"Fleming?"

Startled, she whipped around. A car passed by. The courthouse bell began to toll. And Fleming laughed because she felt ridiculous. Jason Macland stepped off the curb across the street.

"I meant to call you," he said. "I'm sorry about what happened in my office this morning. Are you all right?"

"Fine." She did feel fine now. He'd stepped in front of her with Paige, and now he made her feel safe because she wasn't alone in the streets. She checked herself. How could she ever be afraid in Bliss, the mountain town that was part of her body and blood?

"How about you?" she asked.

His smile was self-deprecating and frustrated at the same time. "Also fine, except you and I will have to talk again. I'm sorry, but we have to discuss your loan."

So—not so much concern for her as for his bank. "I'm gathering the information your assistant emailed about."

"Good. The sooner we settle better terms, the safer your business will be." Jason stepped onto the sidewalk, towering over her, ominous even if he didn't mean to be. "I'm trying to get you into a better position before the rules of your loan take over. I can't help you after that."

"If the loan wasn't legal…"

"That's the problem for all of the people in jeopardy because of Paige. You signed the agreement, so you're responsible for terms that are immoral, but not illegal."

She was caught between worrying he was another bank guy trying to play her, and respecting his honesty. If he was being honest.

She turned, continuing toward the hotel, and somehow, Jason remained with her. "Why are you trying to help me?" she asked. "Why do you care?"

"I'm trying to help anyone who still wants to do business with Macland. It does the bank no good to write off bad loans. Especially as many as they have right now."

*They?* She glanced at him, surprised.

He looked back at her, unbuttoning his top coat button as if he were uncomfortably warm. "We could bring down the local economy."

"How did Mr. Paige manage to fly under the radar?"

"The former bank manager was taking a cut." Jason turned toward the hotel with her, but when she reached for the door he stopped, looking down at her hand.

"I'm having dinner here tonight," she said.

"Oh." He looked back at the square as if he wished he'd planned to be elsewhere.

As they stepped inside, Lyle Benjamin, the hotel's owner, appeared at the top of the cellar stairs, his arms full of wood for the fires that would roar until midnight in the parlor dining room and reception area.

"Not you, too, Fleming?" he asked, glancing from Jason to her.

She blushed, and Jason looked impatient.

"The gossip in this town defeats any need for the internet," he said.

"Sorry." Lyle sent Fleming an apologetic look. "Will your mom be home for the holidays?"

"She and Hugh are on a vacation." A month in a fancy hut in Bora Bora. She couldn't control a smidge of envy for their carefree thirty days. "But they'll be back for Christmas."

"Good to hear it." He carried the wood to the hearth near his check-in counter and tossed a log into the flames. "Table for two?"

"No." Fleming flinched as Jason's voice echoed her own, and they both turned down the opportunity to share a meal.

"I'll call down for room service," he said.

Fleming breathed a sigh of relief. She had to create a battle plan. This man wanted his bank back in the black. He might claim he was helping her, but he'd take Mainly Merry Christmas if shutting her down bettered his bottom line.

# CHAPTER TWO

AFTER A SOLO Thanksgiving dinner in his room the following evening, Jason tried to concentrate on his tablet. He'd just about decided what he could do for Fleming. Next up was a guy who ran one of the last barbershops in America.

All these people were becoming far more than names on electronic files. He'd turned Paige's information over to an assistant DA friend in New York. He wanted someone to make sure the local prosecutor put Paige away for as long as he deserved. Jason had several more weeks to negotiate small-town, Christmas-spirited Bliss.

He feared he wouldn't be the only one who doubted the existence of Santa by the time he finished this favor for his grandfather.

On the up side, he was charging his father top dollar for work that was a lot less complex than his usual contracts.

He stood, stretching the muscles in his back. Voices from downstairs had risen through the old floorboards as families celebrated while he worked. He'd been so focused on his task he'd hardly remembered it was Thanksgiving.

Lights seemed suddenly to dance on the courthouse steps. He crossed to the window. A group of people with glow sticks in Christmassy colors was gathering.

Carolers? He shrugged.

Not that he was hot for singing holiday songs, but he hadn't been outside these four walls all day.

He grabbed his coat and hit the hallway. Downstairs, the lobby was empty. When he went outside, he heard the first strains of "We Wish You a Merry Christmas."

He almost turned back, but a little boy going by waved a shy hello with the hand his mother wasn't holding. Jason didn't have the heart to show his cynical side to someone too young to understand.

Instead, he smiled and waved back.

He didn't cross the square to the carolers, but he walked quickly along the sidewalk. Fresh air. He needed some of that.

Apparently, he was witnessing some kind of Bliss, Tennessee, ritual. Most of the citizens and shop owners appeared to be trailing toward the courthouse. It wasn't until he reached a cotton-swathed window displaying a Christmas village and a running train that he saw another human being not joining in the singing.

He looked up. A rich red sign hung overhead, emblazoned with the words Mainly Merry Christmas. He looked inside again. Fleming, on the wide-plank floor inside, was engrossed in putting together another train track, clearly set to run around a verdant Christmas tree.

Jason tried the door. To his surprise, it opened.

She looked up eagerly at the sound of the sleigh bells above her door. Her face sobered as she saw him.

"What's going on at the courthouse?" he asked.

Her smile was a surprise that made him feel less at loose ends. They shared a puzzling intimacy after yesterday.

"It's tradition." She scrambled to her feet as he shut the cold out behind him. "Everyone goes to the courthouse, and we sing carols to welcome the holiday season. Your bank files must show you we do a lot more business around here this time of year."

"Until spring," he said, "and then there's a slight dip until summer vacationers arrive." He went to get a closer look at the train track. "Need some help?"

She joined him. "I do, but not with this. Why don't we talk about my loan?"

The figures were burned inside his head, but he didn't want to make a mistake. "This isn't a workday. Why aren't you out there singing?"

"I'm maybe weeks away from losing my shop. I have to work today and sell tomorrow." She sat and started placing the track again.

"You could sell this train set and make a sizable sum." His grandfather had a similar one he'd bought at an auction and shared with Jason all the Christmases they'd spent together.

"More tradition."

He retrieved a box of spare track from the window seat and carried it to her. "You could run this all around the store."

"I'm torn between the charm of how that would look and the risk of children stepping on it."

"Take the risk."

She laughed. "Is that the way you feel about loans, as well?"

He shook his head. "I'm afraid not."

"So you come across as all concerned for us, but you'll close us down if you have to?"

He nodded, passing her a straight piece that she laid, directing the track toward a shelf of vintage holiday cards. "I don't always enjoy what I have to do, but I hope you and everyone else here will realize none of my decisions are personal."

"They should be personal. You should be going out of your way to meet these people. We're not in some big city like New York. In a town this small, you have to study each face and family. You should try to understand what's at risk before you start destroying people's lives."

"I'm not destroying anyone. I've told everyone I've seen exactly what I've told you, but I can't fix what's wrong if I don't do what's right for the bank's investors."

"In a town of this size, with a bank this

small, we're all investors," she said, her temper slipping a little, and he had to wonder if the cliché about fiery redheaded women might be true.

"I'm working for my family right now, and they've owned the bank for over a hundred years."

Fleming eyed him as if he didn't quite understand reality. "Not unusual in Bliss. Almost every family out on the square has roots that deep."

"Where's your family?" He had no right to ask, but he wanted to know. She'd told Lyle her mother would be back for Christmas.

"My mother recently married." Fleming's voice softened and warmed in a way that didn't happen in his family. "She'd been dating this guy for a few years, but after I finished college, they married." She looked even more wistful. "I always suspected she stayed here so long because of me, so that I'd have my home to come back to. After she moved to Knoxville to be with Hugh—that's his name—I took over the store."

"And refinanced?" Jason asked.

She nodded. "I had to pay my mom, although now I'm wishing I'd been a little less noble about that." Her grin, as she reached for another piece of track, made him feel as if he knew her.

"I can see that." Fleming must be paying her mother out of what she made each month, as well as paying the bank's note. She was stretched thin, and from what he could tell, the economy in this remote resort had dipped in recent years.

"Why aren't you with family today?" she asked.

He hesitated. Sharing his history spelled involvement, and he wasn't used to getting involved. But he'd asked her a personal question, and he liked that she'd answered. "We don't really do that. I have younger siblings." His father made a habit of marriage. "But they're all in college, or they have families of their own. No one went home this year."

"And you're home here, working?"

"I lived here once," he said.

"I know." She blushed as she pointed to a curving piece of track and started a path around the end of the shelf, getting to her knees. "Lyle told me. He remembers your parents."

"I don't remember being here. They moved when I was really young."

"Maybe Bliss wasn't big enough for them."

For his dad? No. Bliss was no place to run an empire. "He profited by some boom years, and New York suits him better."

"And you?"

Jason hesitated again, but she flipped her long, rich red braid over her shoulder, and she looked sweet and open. Not as if she were searching for a way to read him and use him. That had happened more than once. If he were the marrying kind, he'd be more like his father than he'd like to admit. At least he didn't pretend he was the committing kind.

"I have itchy feet," he said, more honest than he meant to be. "New places challenge me. New jobs."

"I didn't know that many banks could be rescued—or needed rescuing."

"It's not just banks," he said. "I clean up all kinds of ailing companies."

She was on the other side of the shelf, but she leaned back to look at him. "Then why the bank? Sounds as if we're small potatoes."

"Not to my grandfather. This was his pride and joy, and he gave it the foundation that allowed my father to move on. I owe him." For that, and for so much more. More than Jason was willing to admit. He set the box of tracks on the floor where she could reach it. "Speaking of which, I should go. I have some work to look at. What do you say we meet to talk about your business?"

"Sure." She pushed her bangs out of her eyes. "When?"

"And where. I thought you might prefer to meet at the hotel, or a coffee shop, somewhere other than my office."

She got to her feet, clutching the metal track. "I'm not trying to duck you, but I have to work tomorrow. It's a huge day for the shop."

He hated the way people looked at him, as if he were trying to destroy them for a buck. "How about Saturday evening? After you close up? I can come by here."

"Sounds good." She shrugged, but then threw back her shoulders and looked him in the eye. "Just be careful when you go back to your office. Paige might not be the only one who's upset with the bank, and you can't count on Mr. Oakes and his colleague showing up in the nick of time."

# CHAPTER THREE

IF ONLY SHE'D kept her mouth shut. Jason was already reaching for the door when she'd told him to be cautious—as if she knew him at all. As if she had any right, or there were any reason.

"You don't have to be embarrassed, Fleming," he said. "I can see it's bothering you— the loan, the attack…"

"It's this situation. I never understood how hard my mom worked while I flitted around town, dropping off flyers about sales or ornament-making workshops." She was still talking too much, and she needed to put some flyers together.

"We can work this out. A new loan will help you. I'm not sure why I can't convince anyone of that."

"We've been burned." Fleming stacked the track in her hand on top of the pile in the box. Time to stop dressing up the store and get down to business. "It's hard to trust another guy in the same job. I don't mean to be rude, but what you really want is for the problem to go away. We're problems to you."

"What I want is to get back to my own life and the work I've put off to help my grandfather." He didn't stop at the door this time, except to say "I'll see you after you close the shop on Saturday."

The door shut behind him with an ironic jingling of bells.

"Kind of sensitive for a guy whose major function is to shatter dreams." She tried to be ironic, too, but that was a little tricky with a knot of tears in her throat.

ON FRIDAY, the customers flowed like a lovely mountain stream. Saturday, she sold almost as much. And she tucked a flyer for ornament-making classes into each shopping bag.

Unfortunately, she'd forgotten she had to wrap packages after work, for a holiday gift drive. She called Jason's office, deeply aware that meeting after hours was a favor he was doing for her and not a professional requirement. She explained her commitment to Hilda.

"The gifts have to be wrapped in stages," she said. "Or we don't finish them all."

"I know. I have a pile myself that are due at the Women and Children's Shelter on Wednesday." Hilda's voice lowered, as if she was looking away. "Let me check his schedule. I know he wants to see you as soon as possible."

"Well, I'm hardly fragile. I could meet him at his office on Monday morning." Fleming grabbed a couple rolls of wrapping paper and dropped bows into a shopping bag. "Or he can come to my house. You can give him my address."

"I'll do that, but I'll tell him to call or text before he shows up."

"Perfect," Fleming said.

Sort of. Maybe if he came to her home, he'd feel the bond she had with Bliss, Tennessee. The mountains outside her doorway were her strength. She depended on the ridges that somehow looked blue on a misty morning. They didn't leave. They stayed where you needed them. And she loved the store like that, too. She'd do whatever Jason asked of her to keep it. She just needed a chance that was real this time.

IN HIS CAR, Jason plugged in Fleming's address and let the nav system take him out of town. He turned right just past the courthouse, and soon the two-lane road began to climb among dark evergreens, past lit-up chairlifts and trees wreathed with strings of colorful balls that glittered in his headlights.

At a spot where he didn't see a break in the forest, the voice on his navigation system insisted he turn right. Just in time, he saw the narrow road. He turned, and the slim ribbon of pavement shrank even further. The scent of wood smoke filtered into the car. He breathed deep.

The woods closed in around him, but he didn't feel suffocated. He could imagine Fleming running through this almost-winter landscape, her red hair flashing between the trees, her flight as impetuous as her conversation.

If he hadn't come to Bliss to make the lives of several of its citizens miserable, he might better be able to enjoy the beauty of this home he'd never known. Already, down in town, city workers had begun to string holiday lights between lampposts on the streets. A huge Christmas tree was being decorated on the circular concrete piazza in front of the courthouse.

Blinking lights in the woods suggested he'd reached Fleming's place even before his GPS told him to turn. He found her driveway just as the voice in his car gave directions.

Fleming had set up floodlights that shone on the old-fashioned wraparound porch fronting her small farmhouse. She'd looped a strand of Christmas lights along the railing and started on the roof ledge, as well. Smoke curled out of the chimney, gathering above the roofline.

He parked in front of her garage and got out of his car, bringing the ubiquitous tablet with him. His feet crunched on gravel. He breathed deeply the scents of fire and fallen leaves.

Funny how he missed familiar city smells, the occasional stench of garbage on the sidewalk and honking cars.

The door opened and Fleming came out, wrapping her arms around herself against the cold.

"Thanks for coming out here," she said.

"You're in the middle of putting up decorations?"

"I stopped when I couldn't see the roof well

enough to find the nails from last year. And I have to wrap packages tonight."

"Already? They start Christmas early around here."

He started up the stairs. Her smile as he reached her warmed him, and he couldn't help wondering how many women had met their men at this door. This little farmhouse had been here a long time.

"Come in." She reached for his coat as they went inside. "Would you like coffee? A drink? Some cocoa? I have a recipe from my mother. Best hot cocoa ever."

"I've heard that." He nodded.

"That's funny. The details of gossip in my town…" Smiling, she stopped in the living room, where she scooped the files she'd carried into his office from beneath a pile of wrapped packages.

"What are you doing there?" he asked.

"They're for a women-and-children's shelter in town. We used to ask donors to wrap them, but sometimes the gifts weren't appropriate, or someone would give a slightly used present. We're grateful for anything for the shelter, but at this time of year, we like the children to remember how special they are, and a new gift seems to send that message more strongly."

Jason usually gave his assistant a list for his family, and asked her to do the angel gifts some of the department stores offered. "I'll try not to keep you long," he said, following her into the kitchen, a clean gray-blue room that somehow wrapped him in warmth.

A couple of candles scented the air with a faint fragrance of apple, one on the quartz counter and one on the butcher-block island. The flames reflected off the white tiles above the wide sink.

"Have a seat." She motioned toward the stools around the island as she began gathering ingredients. "Or there at the table, if you prefer."

He glanced toward the long, rustic table that fronted a wall of windows. It was too dark now to see the trees.

"You don't need drapes or curtains out here," he said.

"Not on this side of the house, anyway. I probably don't on the front, either." She glanced at him with a rueful grin. "Wednesday night was the first time I've felt anxious in here since I was a teenager."

"I'm sorry for what happened."

"Not your fault." She shook her head. "I shouldn't have said anything. I'm not blaming you. I felt foolish for being afraid."

"No one's ever attacked you at work?" he asked ruefully.

She turned from the fridge, holding a carton of milk. "I hope it's not a common thing for you?"

"I was being sarcastic."

"Good." She poured milk into a saucepan on the stove, but then came to the island and opened her folders. "Help yourself," she said, too trustingly. "I think I have everything."

"Let me check these figures, and then we'll go over the offer I have. If these numbers look different, I'll change things as we go."

She hesitated. "I guess, but Mr. Paige sounded that certain, too, and he turned out to be…"

"I'm not Paige."

She blushed so easily, as if she was as honest and innocent as she sounded.

Jason shook his head, glad when she went back to the stove. He had to halt this attraction now. No more noticing the soft, vulnerable line of her jaw, the richness of her voice. The way she made him feel welcome and wanted, and then was frank enough to admit she might not trust his motives.

She reached for a knob on the stove and a gas flame whooshed beneath the saucepan. The domesticated scene should have put him on his guard. This would normally be the moment he remembered an early meeting or some task he'd forgotten.

He dragged his attention to the tablet, swiping the screen with more firmness than necessary. While Fleming worked, he did, too. His rage at Paige grew, as it did every time he studied one of these files.

"What kind of guy comes to a town like this and robs the people most in need of honest lending?"

"You mean because I'm barely making ends meet?"

"Well." Jason sat back, folding his arms. "Yes. You were a mark to him."

"You know that's not a compliment, right?" She pulled her red silicone spoon out of the saucepan and used a quilted mitt to lift the pan and pour hot chocolate into a tall, wide-mouthed cup.

"It just means I know you can't afford to be cheated."

"But you're asking me to refinance." She filled the other cup, this one as bright red as Santa's gift bag.

"With terms that won't drive you into foreclosure," Jason said.

"So I'm about to take on greater debt again?"

"Not in the long run." He took the mug she handed him, warmed by her touch. She didn't seem to notice him react. "And I hate to suggest this, but you can refinance again when your circumstances improve."

"If they do. If I keep starting over with a new loan, I'll never be able to retire."

Jason laughed, but then hoped she meant it as a joke.

She took the saucepan back to the sink and quickly washed it. "This choice isn't intuitive."

She didn't have much of a choice. Not for the first time, he wished he could make things easier. Not just for her, but mostly for her.

"You're quiet," she said.

"I normally make a plan that will allow a business to succeed. By the time the hard decisions start, I'm on to the next job. Maybe this is why I prefer it that way. I don't like to see your fear or anyone else's."

"I understand you have a job you need to do," she said, "but my mom opened this store when I was a child. We used to make a good living. I'm not sure what's gone wrong, but I do know that the store saved us from poverty. She scraped together the original money and persuaded suppliers they could trust her. And every year, she made everyone in this town remember how magical the holidays are supposed to be."

Jason shrugged. He had a vague memory of trying to be asleep for Santa—but that might be from some TV show he'd watched with his nieces and nephews.

"You never waited for Santa?" Fleming asked. "You never tried to make yourself sleep while you listened for sleigh bells on the roof, because someone convinced you he wouldn't come until you closed your eyes?"

Jason swallowed, uncomfortable with her mind reading. "I guess my family is different than yours. More pragmatic, maybe," he said. "Bankers, almost every one of us."

"My mom's practical. She's had to be."

"What about your dad?" Jason grimaced as he expressed an interest he shouldn't have. "Is he—"

"I don't know what he is." She tucked the cocoa and sugar into a cabinet, wiping the counter so hard Jason was surprised she didn't shave off a layer of stone. "He went out one day for doughnuts, of all things, and never came back." She shook her head. "Well— he came back in a few years and claimed he wanted to make things right. He just never managed to follow through."

And this new guy her mom had married? Jason had the good sense not to ask. "I'm sorry, Fleming. None of my business. What's the opposite of Santa Claus? Because that's who I am."

"I believe that man's name was Scrooge, not Macland. Let's look at the information you brought me."

## CHAPTER FOUR

LOOKING AT JASON'S facts and figures, Fleming felt as if she'd ended up at the top of the naughty list. "I'd love to talk to Mr. Paige about why he did this."

"I've talked to him. He has a story about how the bank didn't set him up with a fair retirement, and he was just providing for his own. Forget about him. You have to concentrate on what you want. Does this store mean as much to you as it did to your mother?"

"Are you suggesting I give it up?" Fleming eyed the numbers on his tablet screen with horror and reached blindly for her hot chocolate. "My mom and I both love that store. I have to find a way to keep it."

He straightened. "For your mother?"

"For me." She had a secret she never shared, not even with her mother. Writing. She'd thought she'd have that and the store, and one would feed the other. She'd been making up stories about their customers since she first stood on a step stool behind the counter.

So far her writing hadn't gone the way she'd dreamed of, but none of her plans included walking away from the store that had been her after-school care, her shelter from the storms of childhood and her summer job each year of college.

It had been her and her mother's place. Like their home. She couldn't walk away.

"Fleming?"

"It matters to me, too, but I didn't actually understand how much business has fallen off this year. How can a shop that caters to Christmas fail in November in a resort town that explodes in population this time of year?"

"Give me a try," he said. "I'll help."

She felt sick. "That's exactly what Mr. Paige said."

"But Paige was lying. I don't lie." Jason dusted his hands on his jeans. "It's business," he said. "The fewer loans we lose, the better off we are."

"I think you're telling me you're giving me more time at a slightly lower interest rate, but

I'll still be paying almost the same amount over the life of the loan."

He nodded. "I want to help you, but I can't actually take a loss on the arrangement."

With shaking fingers, Fleming leafed through the pages of notes and compared the figures he'd jotted down to her income and outgoing debt payments. She got up and grabbed her phone off the island to open the calculator and rerun the equations.

Her cheeks flushed, but she ducked her head and tried to let her hair flow over her face. She could almost feel his longing to get out of here, making the whole situation even more humiliating.

"It's a building," he said. "Not a person. Not a member of your family."

"You say that because you haven't found the place you want to stay. You aren't tied to a building or people." Though Fleming didn't buy that all bankers were that detached.

"I'm asking you to think about this decision, the same way I'll ask everyone else I have to see. If you take on new terms, you'll be putting a lot of money and even more time into a place. You can get another job."

She shook her head stubbornly, trying to

see herself anywhere but in Bliss, doing anything else. Except the writing that was her secret joy, the dream she superstitiously feared shattering if she shared it. "This is who I am."

He sipped his cocoa once, then again, but was so intent on her finances he didn't seem to notice how much he clearly liked the drink she'd made him. "Have you considered carrying different lines from less expensive suppliers? Your profit margin seems to shrink every year."

Her hackles rose. "I can't sell tawdry items. That wouldn't go over in this town. You don't know Bliss."

"You have that right."

"And even if I were positive you're in this with our best interests, rather than the bank's, I can't afford your consulting fee." Fleming ran out of breath. "Sorry. Again. I'm sounding rude, but I'm really trying to be careful. This time."

"I keep trying to make you see the bank won't survive if its customers fail." Standing, Jason took his jacket off the back of his chair. "You don't trust me, and I don't blame you, but talk to someone you do trust, and let me know what you decide."

Maybe she could breathe deeply again without him in her house. He picked up his cup and headed toward the sink, but she took it from him. Washing her dishes was absolutely beyond the scope of his job description.

"You've been here three weeks, Jason. You know people actually choose Bliss as a place to have fun?"

Jason looked over his coffee cup at Lyle. "When there's snow on the slopes, I assume?"

"They're making snow right now. You could take a car up the mountain and ski back down." Lyle waited until Jason put his cup down, and refilled it.

"Thanks. I don't think so."

"Afraid one of the hundreds of people who've paraded through your office at the bank will follow you up there and shove you off? I heard what happened the day before Thanksgiving."

"That was different. Paige lost his retirement fund."

"He took funds from a lot of people. You can't make it right for everyone."

Jason pushed his chair back. "People tell you things, Lyle."

"We're a small community. We tell each other everything—except our secrets. But someone always discovers them and tells those, too."

"No one's told you I'm not here to make things right. I'm here to do a job for my grandfather and move on."

"I remember your grandfather."

That wasn't information Jason felt inclined to investigate. He didn't remember this place. He didn't necessarily want to remember it later. The only important thing he needed to know was that when he left, his father would make sure a decent loan officer and bank manager took over.

"Thanks for breakfast." Jason stood up, sliding his phone into his pocket. "I'm going out for a while."

"Sure." Lyle smirked a little, as if to say he didn't mind a dismissal.

Jason felt like what he was. Rude, uncomfortable, and maybe pushed a little too far, because he didn't know how to react to people here, who didn't outwardly want to use him. Unlike his father.

He started down the sidewalk, his pace as fast as it would have been in New York. After he weaved around the third stroller, he realized he was racing with himself. At the same time, he almost ran into a harried father holding on to two children and an oversize shopping bag.

Jason caught the shop door that almost hit one of the boys. Toy store. For once, maybe he could choose his own gifts. He knew where to buy wrapping paper and bows and tape, and Fleming could also tell him where to deliver his packages.

Every shop in Bliss seemed to smell as if someone had just baked an apple pie in it. Did the scent of apple pie prompt people to part with their money?

He took a basket from the stack by the door and started by filling the bottom with small cars. Even he could wrap an undersized square. He chose a few foam puzzles and some cylindrical barrels of building logs. He'd loved those things when he was a kid. He'd built ranches for his superhero action figures to live on.

They made superheroes smaller these days. After he topped the basket off with them, he took his purchases to the counter.

"Whoa," said the young guy waiting to check him out. "Big family?"

"Sort of. Can I leave these here and finish?"

"Sure." He started unloading. "We'll push them all to the end until you come back."

Jason had one more thing he wanted to buy. He loved trains as much as Fleming did. His grandparents had given him one every year. He still had them packed away. Somewhere.

He chose a wooden one, like the one he loved best. The cars were hand painted. Each fitted neatly to its mate via wooden couplings. The train ran on a wooden track that made a neat series of wide turns, accommodating play for a young child not yet completely in charge of dexterity.

Shopping bags in hand, he went on to Mainly Merry Christmas, passing both a card store and a stationery shop that probably carried a wide selection of paper and ribbons.

Fleming looked up from her open laptop when the bells jingled above his head.

"What are you doing here?" she asked.

He smiled at her. "Nice to see you, too."

She grinned, her embarrassment kind of

charming. "I meant, welcome. What can I do for you?"

"I need a few things."

"You have a few things." She pointed to the bag. "Getting to your Christmas shopping early?"

Her soft mockery left him a little tongue-tied. "I was thinking last night, while you were wrapping your gifts…"

Fleming came around the counter, her smile a welcome into her community the likes of which he'd never been offered. "You bought some things for the shelter?"

"I always ask my assistant to write a check or choose a charity, or even to buy gifts for those trees in the department stores."

"Oh."

"You made me feel ashamed last night," he said.

"I doubt anyone cares how the gifts arrive."

"Maybe not." He lifted the bag onto the counter. "But I thought I could put in a little effort."

"I like to see a rich guy trying to walk in normal shoes."

"I'm not that rich." But just for a second, he wasn't himself. He wished he could offer some of his own money to ease the holiday suffering he was causing here in Bliss.

"Let me donate wrapping paper," she said.

"Fleming, are you insane?" He walked so close to her that his breath stirred the red strands around her face. "You can't afford to give me paper. I'll buy enough to wrap these, and some bows and those little cards."

She laughed, but then hurried around the counter to a tree, where she touched a shiny, hard plastic candy cane. "If you wanted, you could add a little ornament to the bows. Nothing breakable, but something a child might keep for her own home next year."

He hardly heard because he was so busy taking in Fleming's happy face. She might tempt a man to believe in magical holidays.

"You choose," he said.

She shook her head, touching his arm with her fingertips. "I'll help you."

He wanted to cover her hand and pull it to his mouth, to feel her soft skin against his lips and learn what she would say if she knew how her happy warmth touched him.

Instead, he completed his purchases, took his bags and left, reminding her to read the refinancing paperwork he'd given her.

FLEMING CLOSED THE shop early after Jason left, barely managing not to press her face to the door and watch him walk away. He would not be staying, she reminded herself. He'd always walk away.

And she had to focus on her own work. Sadly, no one was fighting to come inside the shop. Maybe they'd seen her collaborating with the enemy and hadn't wanted to join them.

She locked the back door behind her and walked to her car, shivering in the cold night air. What she wouldn't give for one more of those years when she and her mother had held the doors open during the first post-Thanksgiving week until ten or eleven at night.

This year, with an über-efficient businessman putting fear in everyone who'd fallen behind on one of Paige's loans, people seemed to have locked up their wallets. Her business was an easy luxury to cut.

Driving home, she took comfort from the decorations going up in the heart of town. Snowflakes on Victorian streetlamps. Wire-and-light Santas and snowmen waving from the corners. Eight tiny reindeer grazing on the grassy areas of the courthouse square.

Even as she plunged into the darkness of the country roads she passed signs of the coming holidays. The Hadleys' fence sparkled with loops of twinkling red and green lights. Blue and white stars loomed on the Petersons' iron gates. The Bradleys' Christmas-tree farm was an oasis of holiday decor, inviting passersby to stop in and choose a tree of their own.

Fleming pushed her anxiety to arm's length. She'd read the refinancing contracts. She hadn't called her mother during what was essentially a honeymoon. She had to refinance or give up the store, and that wasn't a choice.

All her anxiety had given her a plan for the pages she needed to write tonight, a scene that cried out for the emotion she was fighting so hard not to feel in real life.

She turned in at her driveway, pausing to collect the mail from the black metal box that still bore the dents from an unfortunate mailbox-baseball incident on Halloween. She should replace it, but every little penny...

ON THURSDAY MORNING, Fleming waited outside Jason's office, uncertain whether she was more anxious about seeing him or dealing with the loan.

Voices rose loudly inside the office. Instantly concerned that someone else might be attacking Jason, Fleming glanced at Hilda, who grimaced and stared at her phone. "I have 911 on speed dial now," the woman said.

"I'm sorry you have to. It's just a bad time of year for this to happen."

Hilda scrunched up her eyebrows. "But if he'd waited, some people would have lost their homes and businesses."

"I'm one of them," Fleming said without thinking.

"What a mess."

The office door opened and Jason came out, his arm across the shoulders of a man in coveralls. Fred Limber, who owned a tire shop a few blocks from the square.

"So don't worry. I'll send you the terms. I don't see any reason you can't meet this obligation, Fred, and if you have problems, you get in touch with me."

"I can't afford your advice on my business, Jason."

"My name is on this bank." Jason wiped his free hand down his leg, as if it were sweating. "I can spare you the time."

Fleming stood, and both men looked at her.

Jason's gaze, warm with a smile, made her heart seize in a funny, clenching cramp. She smoothed the skirt of her navy shift dress.

He didn't believe in Santa? With his offers to help the people who were in trouble thanks to Mr. Paige, it was like he was carrying around a big old sack of gifts.

Fred turned and shook Jason's hand. "Sorry for yelling at you."

"Sorry for yelling back."

"I'll read those papers and talk to my brother. He's an accountant. Then I'll set up an appointment with Hilda."

"Good. We'll see you then." Jason walked Fred to the door, and after he shut it, he leaned against the heavy wood for a second. He might pretend to be detached, but clearly, walking away from the problems he was making for people in Bliss was not as easy as he might have thought. He smiled at Fleming, and then rubbed his hand over his mouth. "I know you don't make coffee, Hilda—"

"No, I don't."

"But—"

"Just this once." She rose from behind her desk. "Want one, Fleming?"

With brandy, for goodness' sake. "Yes, please."

"I'll bring it in."

Jason went into his office and Fleming followed.

"Where do we start?" he asked.

No need to beat around the bush. "I'm going to save the store."

"Are you sure?" He took a stack of papers from his desk and then came to the sofa, where she'd already taken the same seat she'd occupied the other day.

"Maybe I can help you, too." He lifted the first page and glanced toward the doorway. "Like with Fred," he said.

It seemed clear that he was trying to tell her he didn't care more for her than he should. She was just another victim of the bank's bad loan officer.

She knew Jason's plans. He was leaving town as soon as he finished this unwelcome favor.

"I'm happy to take advice," Fleming said, purposefully rejecting the idea that it would come straight from him.

"I have a few suggestions."

"But you won't be here." She closed her

eyes briefly, determined to fight her own inner demons. Since the day her father had walked out of her life, she'd mistrusted men in authority. And yet let a guy go out of his way to help someone, and she couldn't restrain herself from being attracted. "And I can't entirely trust a bank that agrees I can afford their loan."

"I'm not pretending it will be easy, but maybe we can streamline your processes in the shop to save some overhead. Spend more wisely."

She lifted her chin. "The shop is still mine. I make the decisions."

"You have three days to change your mind, Fleming. Don't let the deadline pass."

# CHAPTER FIVE

AFTER ENDURING FRED'S shouting and Fleming's prickly mood, Jason ducked past the registration desk in the hotel that night. It usually took a few weeks for him to get this anxious to leave a work site.

He'd made a mistake. He should have stayed downstairs and asked if he had unexpected company, because a tall, thin woman in a worn dress was waiting beside his door. She blushed and smiled at him, but tears welled in her eyes.

"Mr. Macland?"

"Jason," he said automatically.

"I'm Rachel Limber."

"Fred's wife?" Should he brace for a fight or help her down the stairs?

She held out a Santa-decorated tin. "I make homemade fudge," she said. "It's really good, and right now it's pretty much all we have to offer as a thank-you."

"Oh." He took the metal container and shook her hand at the same time. "You didn't have to go to the trouble."

"I wanted to. Fred came home hopeful, and for that, I owe you. That old shop of his is mud and oil and nasty smells, but only to me. To him, it's his favorite place in the whole world. I don't know what he'd do if he lost it."

That sounded familiar. Fleming had said the same thing—how many times? "I guess some walls and a place with memories can matter that much, Mrs. Limber."

"It does to Fred. I was ready to give up and move to Knoxville, but our family's here."

Jason smiled. "Remind Fred he can call me or email anytime."

"Thanks." She looked at him closely. "I knew your grandmother."

His grandparents had sold their home and moved to New York to help with Jason. Their support had become ever more vital to his father, who'd managed to retain custody of Jason's younger sisters and brother as he divorced their mothers.

Robert Macland's parents had given the family stability. Safety.

"I don't think she ever came back here.

She or my grandfather." Jason had taken his grandparents so much for granted that he'd never thought to ask if they missed the place.

Why hadn't he asked? Self-absorption must be a genetic trait.

"I wish she had. She was good friends with my mom. I know she would have been welcome." Rachel Limber hooked her purse more securely over her arm and turned toward the stairs. "People shouldn't disappear from each other's lives. That's what I hate most about this bank thing. You're helping Fred, but you were too late for some."

He nodded. "My grandfather asked me to come and to move quickly."

"Good people, your grandparents, but we all knew your father. This little world was never going to be big enough for him. Merry Christmas, Jason. I hope I'll see you around town."

He stared after her, listening to the clack of her heels on the wooden stairs. Hadn't he said almost the same thing about his father to Fleming? The small town of Bliss seemed to be closing in on him.

In his suite, Jason tossed the big key that weighed down his jacket pocket onto a table in front of the fireplace. He set the tin of fudge beside it.

Aromas from downstairs drifted up. His stomach growled as he glanced at the mail. He considered phoning down for dinner, but then rejected the idea, striking a long match to the logs and kindling waiting on the hearth.

He turned back to the stack of letters that he'd collected from his temporary post office box. Even in an age where a man did most of his correspondence via email, he still received a bundle of mail most days.

A long, lavender envelope caught his eye. Not the envelope, but the penmanship. Fat, round writing that was familiar because he'd read every line in every one of the day planners his mother had left behind when she'd abandoned him and his father. He stared at the name on the return address: Teresa Macland Brown.

It left him feeling as dazed as if he'd stormed headfirst into a wall.

His mother had written to him?

She'd hardly ever bothered. No cards, no emails, though he'd written to her almost the first moment he'd set up his own email address. He'd searched for her contact information on his father's computer.

Secretly. Because Robert had been so angry at his wife's disappearance that he had discouraged Jason from trying to get in touch with her. He'd reminded Jason regularly that she would only hurt him again.

Jason had never forgotten that last morning with her.

After an earsplitting argument between his parents, Jason's mother had called a porter to take her luggage down to the street, and then she'd left. Jason sneaked into the elevator of their Manhattan loft to follow her, but she didn't even wait for her bags. She was running out of the building's other elevator as the doors opened on Jason's.

He hurried after her, but when he reached the glass doors in the lobby, someone tall grabbed his shoulders and jerked him back.

"Careful, son, that's a busy street out there." It was the doorman.

Jason's mother had run, sobbing, into the arms of a pale-haired man. He'd tipped up her face and wiped at her cheekbones with his thumbs. Then he'd kissed her with a tenderness that made Jason feel sick, because the man wasn't his dad.

The runaway couple had scrambled into a waiting cab as if they couldn't escape fast enough. With a jolt, the vehicle had started forward, and his mother and the stranger had disappeared into the flow of traffic.

She'd never looked back.

She'd hardly ever called. Initially, his father had tried to make excuses for her. For that, Jason had been grateful, but that image of her grabbing her new man and running away from their life stuck in his head even today.

No explanations had ever been necessary. She hadn't loved his father or him enough to stay. His dad said staying in one place wasn't her thing, and he couldn't blame her for that when he suffered from the same affliction. But Jason had never understood what he'd done to make her leave him, too.

Finally, he'd told his dad he understood that his mother didn't love him, and they'd never discussed her again. She'd called once or twice, and they'd talked like strangers. Then they'd stopped talking at all.

Tightening his jaw, Jason finally opened the ridiculously feminine envelope. A single page slid out onto the floor. He picked it up. Heavy writing had impressed the pale purple paper with a few lines that showed through the back of the sheet. He needn't have dreaded a long explanation, or an excuse.

But how had she known where to find him? How long had she been keeping tabs on him?

He unfolded the piece of paper. She wrote the way she'd talked all those years ago, as if she still didn't have a lot to say. Just his name, a diffident request to meet, "I want to talk to you," and her phone number.

He'd had more emotional communication from the bank's frightened clients. He dropped the brief note and envelope on a side table with his keys.

After all these years, that was her best effort?

Why now? Why here?

How badly did he want to know?

He changed into running clothes and headed downstairs. The slap of his shoes against the sidewalk felt good. The stretch of his muscles as he ran and the cold air biting into his face reminded him he was alive. He was working. Nothing here was permanent. He just had to keep running to put everything back into perspective.

But then he came to Fleming's shop, where she was stringing lights along the window. For a second, he considered running on past, but he couldn't leave her standing on a chair to handle the lights alone.

He stopped, breathing hard enough to cause a cloud of steam to form in front of his face. Fleming, tangled in lights, stared at him as if to ask what he wanted.

If she'd asked out loud, he wouldn't have known how to answer. He wasn't even certain how he'd ended up in the one place she was sure to be. "Why don't you let me help you?"

She looked down at him, considering. "I can do this by myself."

Ignoring her stubbornness, he put his hand on the back of the chair. "Do we really need this?" He reached up to the metal frame of the awning in front of Mainly Merry Christmas. It was about four inches higher than his fingertips. "I guess we do."

He took off his hoodie so he could see what he was doing and traded places with Fleming on the chair, noticing as they passed each other, just shy of touching, that she couldn't look away from him any more than he could tear his gaze from her.

Slowly, she handed him a roll of green duct tape that matched the awning. She'd been using it to fasten the light cords to the canvas. She lifted the string of lights, and he took it, leaning back to see how she'd been lining them up.

"Why are you angry with me, Fleming?"

"I'm not." She said it in such a rush it was obviously untrue. "I'm sorry. Maybe I am lashing out a little, because I find myself in a bad situation."

"You can afford this loan. You won't lose the store."

"Why are you so helpful? You act as if the bank's at fault."

"I guess it is." He probably shouldn't say that. "According to the attorneys, Paige kept the loans just this side of legal so they'd go through the system. He'll be going to jail because he got greedy enough to skim the profits."

"Otherwise, the bank would have been part of his scam," she said.

"I guess my family does have a level we won't stoop below." Jason smiled, but he wasn't entirely joking. "I'm helping you and everyone else he cheated because it's the right thing to do, and it's best for this town if all of you can continue to do business with Macland's."

"Now you sound like a commercial," she said, with a smile that made him feel less insulted, more as if they were back on the shaky footing of their unacknowledged attraction.

"That burns a lot more than being called heartless."

"You're imagining things." Briskly, she handed him the last of the lights, and he put them up, secured them with the heavy-duty tape, and then stepped off the chair.

"Want to turn them on?"

Nodding, she went inside and threw a switch. The lights began to twinkle just as a snowflake landed on his cheek. He looked up and saw blue-gray sky, but when he turned his head to look at the courthouse behind him, he saw more flakes, thickening in the air.

"Snow," he said, as the shop bells jangled and Fleming rejoined him.

"About time. That should help everyone in business up here."

He searched her face, impressed that he'd never heard panic in her voice, even the day she'd agreed to sign the loan.

"I swear you're going to be okay," he said, taking her hand. "I took into account the slow times. You're in this for the long haul. If you were only looking to make a quick profit and turn the place over to a new owner, we would have discussed different terms."

She nodded, tears pooling in her eyes. Her throat moved as she tried to swallow, and he pulled her closer still, wrapping one arm around her.

"Until you close on the loan, nothing is permanent."

"I need to close. My life here is permanent." She pressed her cheek to his chest. She was warm and alive and unguarded on this cold day, and she needed his comfort.

It was a potent combination, but when she said the word *permanent*, it reminded him who she was. He couldn't tip up her face and kiss the generous mouth that haunted him when he should have been busy with his own plans. He couldn't put his other arm around her and pretend they could be more than friends.

He did hit-and-run relationships with a mastery he'd learned at his father's knee. Fleming was not a temporary kind of woman.

"Let me take your chair inside before it gets wet," he said.

"I hope the snow now is a good sign for more to come." She held the door, and he carried the chair past her.

Fleming followed him inside, but the bells on the door didn't sound as cheery as now.

"You know, I don't think you're heartless." She went to the front window of the store as if looking for customers to drag inside. "No one here thinks you're heartless."

"Have you been gossiping?" He went to the tall, silver coffeepot she kept behind the counter and poured two cups. He passed one to her, making no effort to avoid contact.

She put one finger through the handle and wrapped her other hand around the cup's rim. He couldn't help noticing every little thing she did.

"Maybe it's gossip," she said. "Maybe people are grateful, and we've talked about it over the doughnut case in the bakery and the egg fridge in the grocery store. When you first arrived, you were all rules and regulations, even when you were sorry you had to do the right thing for the bank."

"I may still have to do that." But he wasn't sanguine as he thought of the number of loans he still had to study.

"You're accidentally getting to know us, and business as usual isn't as easy as it's been in the past."

"You're right about that. I didn't expect to be treated as if I belonged here. People take me at face value." He moved away from her, fingering the thick batting that nestled the miniature village in faux snow in the window. "But I am still the bank's representative."

"I haven't forgotten you'll put the bank ahead of us."

"If I have to, but I didn't with your loan."

"That's what I don't understand about you. You obviously cared about Fred, and I know you've been considerate of me, but if the bottom line creeps up, that's where your attention will go."

"It's my job."

"Your job," she said. "That's your first priority, isn't it?"

He met her measured gaze, knowing she

wouldn't let him put his arm around her now if he tried. "The job is why I'm here."

"I won't let myself forget again." She took her cup to the counter. "But aren't you ever tempted to find out if you could belong somewhere?"

"Fleming—"

"I know," she said. "It's none of my business."

"You're content here in these mountains. I'm not asking you why you aren't tempted by everything you'd find outside this world."

"Because I belong. My life here is a suit of clothes that fits. You haven't found that outfit for yourself." She opened her laptop. "And I don't think you'll allow yourself to look."

"Just like I don't believe you're capable of opening your eyes to anywhere else."

"And now we're getting personal. That's a mistake." Her fingers flew over the keyboard. "I'm asking the attorney for a closing date."

And shutting him out. Making sure he knew she wasn't open to any relationship that might take her away from her beloved mountain home.

"Good," he said. "The sooner you commit to your business, the better." He looked at his watch, not even seeing it. "I should get back to work, too. Good night, Fleming."

"Night."

Her cheery voice irritated him. He set his cup on her counter and looked at her, not hiding his awareness of what they were truly saying to each other. She belonged here. He was leaving.

Neither spoke again as he exited the store and walked away.

FLEMING FELT THE silence in the shop as if it were a pillow smothering her. She sent her email to the bank's loan attorney and closed the laptop, not even tempted to open her story file for a change.

Her heart felt a little broken. She and Jason had talked a lot since she'd first met him in his office that day. They'd never been as personal or as honest as in these last few moments.

She'd met other men, been interested in other men, but laughed to herself now, recognizing that she'd never felt like this before. Attracted, afraid, grateful for the sound of his voice, at a loss when he left her.

But she'd always been clear about where

she stood, where she'd stand forever. In Bliss, her home.

Her phone rang, startling her as it vibrated in her pocket. She reached for it and tears burned in her eyes. "Mom," she said, answering.

"Am I too late? Why haven't you called me?"

Fleming picked up her coffee cup and carried it to the back room, where she put it in the sink. "The grapevine got hold of you?"

"I've heard a few things. Is it true about the loan?"

"Absolutely true, but everything's fine. I have a new one that I'll be able to cover, and the shop will be fine."

"I don't care about the shop." Her mother paused. "Right now, anyway. You sound sad."

"No." Fleming lied as she never had to her mother before. She couldn't explain that her heart had gotten involved without her permission. "I'm fine. Where are you calling from?"

Her mom didn't answer.

"Hello?" Fleming glanced at the phone. It was a long way to a beach hut, but the call remained connected.

"I asked Hugh if we could come home

early. Just a few days. I'm on my way from Knoxville right now. I hope you won't be upset with me for being concerned, but we both thought you might need me."

Fleming didn't know how to respond. "I'm twenty-four, Mom, not a child. Hugh will think—"

"That I wanted to see my daughter. He's part of our family now, too. He understands what the shop means to us both. Besides, he's excited about getting back to the hospital in the morning. Who knows how cardiology might have changed since the great Dr. Belford tempted fate by taking a vacation?"

Her mom was rightly proud of her new husband, who'd never go out for pastry and disappear. "Thank him for me," Fleming said, "and be careful getting here. It's starting to snow."

"Oh, that'll be good for business."

## CHAPTER SIX

FLEMING HAD ALL BUT tackled her mother when she arrived at home the night before. Over hot chocolate and oatmeal cookies, they'd discussed what had happened with the shop and the loan, and then they'd gone to bed.

In the morning, Fleming woke to the smells and sounds of breakfast. She jumped out of bed and ran down the stairs. Her mother turned from the stove, where she was frying bacon.

"I thought pancakes and bacon and coffee and some fresh fruit," she said. "How's that with you?"

"Amazing. I usually just grab an apple or a boiled egg. Even your coffee smells better than mine."

"Help yourself." Katherine went to the fridge and took out pancake batter she'd already mixed. "We should be eating in about ten minutes."

Fleming rubbed her stomach. "Can't be soon enough."

"Now tell me what you're doing to bring up sales in the store."

"I've distributed flyers for an ornament-making workshop. I haven't decided what I want to do so it's pretty vague, but I'll provide the materials as part of the cost."

"I wondered if you'd keep up with the ornament tradition. You should do one each week."

"I was thinking papier-mâché. My friend Julia did some in art school. She might help me come up with something."

"Would she consider running the workshop?"

"We could share the profits if she's willing. I have the shop and she has the skills. She might even be able to put on other classes during the year."

"I'd talk to her," Katherine said. "Call her after breakfast."

"I will. Actually, I kind of have an idea. You know the special ornaments we do each year? I modeled the ones for this year on the snowflakes the town puts on the streetlights." They were 3-D stars with six sides, made so that each leg formed a diamond point. "What if we did something like that, only in jewel colors, with varnish? Nothing ornate—these would be for the children."

"Might be worth the effort if it brings in shoppers."

"And their little ones. We'll keep it easy so the children can be involved in making them."

"Good idea. You should try."

Fleming smiled. "That wasn't so hard for a few minutes of work."

Maybe she'd been putting all her creativity into her writing. Writing her mother didn't even know about. Her own little secret.

"Don't rest your brain now. You'll need more of that kind of work," Katherine said.

"If you have ideas, I'm open to them."

Fleming set silverware and plates on the table. Her mother brought the pancakes and bacon.

"I could stay until you feel better about handling the business and the new loan."

"You could, and I appreciate the offer, but you have a life with Hugh. I'll call you if I have questions. I'm so glad to see you, but I feel guilty that you've come all this way, and ended your vacation early."

Her mom grinned. "Don't. I'm not sure Hugh and I are vacation people. Remember, all you have to do if you need help is call me, and I'll be on my way."

Katherine reached out and squeezed Fleming's hand. "I'm a little worried that you've committed to this because you feel as if you owe me the store. You don't. It was my dream, not yours."

"It's part of all the Christmases we ever had, Mom. Part of the thread of my life. I want the store. And someday, if you and Hugh come home to this house, after he retires, you may be so bored you'll want the business back."

Katherine laughed. "I can't actually deny that." She sat, tucking her napkin in her lap. "I'm glad I came."

"So am I. Stay a day or two, and we'll visit, if Hugh doesn't mind. You always restore my faith in myself."

Faith that Jason had shaken, not because he was cruel or meant to hurt her, but because he was, himself, a pragmatic, practical businessman who'd shown her she'd been complacent and trusted the wrong person.

JASON WAS WALKING to a lunch meeting when he saw the chalkboard on an easel outside Mainly Merry Christmas: Make a Blissful Ornament. Papier-mâché. Classes Inside."

He lifted both brows. Not a bad idea. Something for parents and children to do together. Something for Christmas.

A gust of wind burned his eyes. He tried to imagine living here, being part of this community. It was easier to imagine his sisters and brother having families. Bringing some sort of Macland tradition back here with the kind of marriage his grandparents still kept alive.

But his grandparents were the exception, not the rule of Macland marriages. No one in his family would be coming back here. And he wouldn't be staying.

He sped up, his feet eating up the sidewalk. Thoughts of his mother and her note came to mind. She was family. He hadn't even tried to see her.

She hadn't tried to see him, either, when he'd needed her most, but suddenly, for the first time in a long time, he wondered why. It wasn't that he'd love to forgive and forget, but a guy who spent most of his life uncovering answers to troubling problems shouldn't have been so content to just let the years slide by.

Something about the holidays must be getting under his skin. He glanced at Fleming's sign again.

A car slid to the curb at Jason's side. A luxury SUV. A man rolled down the window.

"Jason, I thought that was you. Glad I made it in time for our appointment." Gabe Kaufman, a client who happened to be driving from Knoxville to Asheville, climbed out of his car. "I'm glad you could see me."

Jason felt for the phone in his overcoat pocket. "I've got your files. Let's talk."

He walked the guy over to a little restaurant behind the square. A server seated them at a linen-covered table, brought a silver carafe of coffee and unobtrusively served a five-star lunch while they discussed Gabe's trading business. They finished the details about the same time dessert arrived, a chocolate mousse confection that took Jason's mind off work for the first time since they'd sat down.

"What are you doing out here?" Gabe

asked. "It's a cute little place, and I can't believe you have access to dining like this." He looked around the smoke-scented, low-beamed room. "But why have you buried yourself in the Tennessee mountains at this time of the year? You don't even have convenient access to an airport."

Jason allowed himself a small smile. Gabe was an important client, but they weren't such close friends that he'd be sharing his family's business with him. "I lived here when I was a kid. I'm just home for a visit."

"Seriously?" Gabe made a big show of his disbelief. "I never knew that. I thought you were Beekman Place, born and bred."

"I spent most of my childhood there, but my roots are here." Nothing had ever sounded more foreign to him. Or less true. He'd never had roots. He didn't need roots like most of mankind. He needed the next challenge. "Everyone goes home once in a while. What are you doing in Asheville for the holidays?"

"The music scene," Gabe said. "My oldest daughter plays a violin. Well—" he swallowed hard "—apparently, it's a fiddle now. If I could tell you the money I've paid for lessons… But she suddenly loves bluegrass, and she heard there was good music here. My wife wanted to spend some time away from the city where there was a chance our phones wouldn't work.

"And you know what? She succeeded. Here I am, and my phone is useless at the place where we're staying. The wife did a little recon trip ahead of our family holiday, and she chose this chalet where she couldn't get reception anywhere on the grounds."

Jason laughed, commiserating. "No one understands a guy who can't relax." Women just assumed such men ran from one place to the next to avoid commitment. Like Fleming… But no—he had to get her out of his head. "Has your family gone to Asheville ahead of you?"

"We've been there a few days, but they came with me today. They seemed to think I might get distracted and not show up back at our equivalent of a desert island." Gabe's smile was wry, as if he was only about half as impatient with his downtime as he was pretending to be. "I dropped them back at that little holiday shop. Can you imagine anything as hopeless as running a store devoted to Christmas year-round? I might beat myself to death with one of the ceramic Santa Clauses in the window."

To his surprise, a surge of irritation stiffened Jason's spine. "It does all right for business," he said, as if there were some good financial reason for him to lie about Fleming's store being in the peak of good fiscal health.

"Yeah? You know the people who run it? Maybe the snow and the ski resorts put visitors in mind of Christmas. So how do people keep busy up here in summer?"

Good question. Jason had no answer. His mind went blank, as if he didn't know how to have fun. He usually worked. For fun, he'd started flying lessons last summer. One year, he'd done some work in Hawaii and dived in the clear waters every free moment he could find. "What do you do anywhere in summer? Whatever's available, I guess." He glanced at the discreet crowd of would-be customers milling quietly by the door. "We might be taking more than our allotted share of time here."

He dropped a wad of cash for lunch on the table and stood, leaving Gabe no choice but to follow. On the street, Jason put out his hand to shake his client's. "It's been good seeing you. Study the files I emailed you, and call me with your questions."

"Oh, no, you don't. You're not running out as if you can't afford a few minutes off the clock. Come down to the little store with me. I want you to meet my wife and girls."

Another great idea. Fleming had made her position pretty clear during their last uncomfortable meeting. Jason made a show of checking his watch. "I don't know..."

"Forget it." Gabe pounded his back as if they were old football teammates. "The global economy won't collapse if you take your eye off it for a few minutes."

Without ever actually agreeing to go, Jason found himself walking with Gabe to the store. He even stepped in front of his friend and opened the door, which was wreathed in hand-drawn candy canes.

Gabe entered ahead of him, but stopped so suddenly Jason thudded into his back. Then he caught sight of the chaos. The door was the only clean thing left in Mainly Merry Christmas.

Three girls and two small boys, all covered in white goop, along with two women who apparently had some connection to the shrieking children, seemed to be wrapping mummies at the small table opposite the cash registers. Their animated voices drowned out Fleming's attempt to calmly instruct them. A third woman had given up to retire, laughing, behind the checkout area.

Fleming caught sight of Gabe and Jason, and said something that got lost in the racket. From her look of consternation, Jason had to assume she wasn't rejoicing at his arrival. Nearly encased in papier-mâché herself, she squared her shoulders, smoothed the white stuff off her hands onto the newspaper-covered table and smiled.

"Good afternoon. May I help you?"

Jason, bemused, didn't have to answer. The two smallest girls bolted for Gabe and pummeled his suit with their sticky hands, shouting "Daddy!" with the elation of children who'd thought their father might have disappeared forever.

One of the women looked at Fleming, her body language an expression of sheer helplessness. Fleming dampened a length of paper towel in a plastic tub of clean water and passed it to her.

"Gabe," the woman said, "maybe we should stay here in Bliss tonight. I think we've got the hang of this papier-mâché thing, and the girls want to finish their ornaments."

The older daughter, clearly bored and nowhere near as coated in goop and glue, shook her head. "I don't."

"The girls want to finish their ornaments," her mother said again. Then she lifted both hands, sticky still, and now slightly fluffy with paper-towel remnants. "And so do I."

"Then, by all means." Gabe turned toward Jason. "Maybe you could give me directions to a good hotel?"

"Sure." Jason brought up the web page for Lyle's place and texted a link to Gabe's phone. "You can call and arrange for a room. Or just walk down the block. It's on the right at the end of the square."

"Go ahead, Gabe," his wife said. "We'll meet you over there after we finish."

"Jason, this is Anita. Anita, my friend Jason. And these are my daughters. Starting with the tallest and least interested in hanging out with the family," he said, grinning with affection, "Delia. And this one—" he flattened his hand in the air above a small, glue-laden head of brown hair "—is Kay. Last but not least, this limpet on my leg is Georgina."

The small redhead clung to him with all her gluey might. "Daddy, I come with you."

"After you finish your art project," Gabe said with justifiable reluctance. "Jason, join us for dinner tonight."

He should welcome the break. Some time with people who didn't owe his family or the bank anything and had no reason to resent him. But he dreaded more questions, and he suspected Fleming and her store might be a topic of dinner-table talk now that Gabe and his family had met her. "Thanks," he said, "but—"

Without thinking, he glanced at Fleming, and she ran her fingers through her hair, streaking it with white. She took a moment to decide to take mercy on him, but then came to his rescue. "Actually, Jason and some friends and I have plans for tonight. We're planning…" She stopped, her blank expression certainly not helping Jason's cause. "A Christmas thing. On the square. Caroling." She finished with a look of triumph.

Gabe's smile was crooked with disbelief. He glanced at Jason assessingly, as if he couldn't decide how best to make fun of him. "Okay. See you in a while. Anita, hose the kids down before you let them be seen in public, will you?"

He hit the sidewalk, wiping at his suit.

His wife made a face at his back as he walked away. "He was joking." She dampened her hands again with the clear water. "I think."

"Jason, why don't you come make an ornament?" Fleming asked, with irony in her voice as if she expected him to say no to the possibility of participating in something fun. "We're doing a test run today, but we're thinking our methods need a little work. Let us try some changes on you." She waved toward the young woman behind the cash register. "This is Julia Walker. She's our instructor for today."

"Julia." He couldn't help doubting her skills, because the place was covered in glue and globs of wet paper. He looked back at Fleming with a nod. Did she think she could scare him off with a challenge?

She came around the counter, rubbing her hands together like a mad scientist on a bad television show. "We may have to turn these snowflakes into snowmen. Here we go again."

"OF COURSE YOU turn out to be a papier-mâché prodigy," Fleming said later that afternoon, as she scooped the last of the glue off the table with a scraping tool Julia had lent her before she'd left for a dinner date.

Jason twirled his ruby-colored ornament above her head. "I think I'll lacquer this." He held it out to her. "You want it?"

Somehow, his not wanting to keep it made her feel as if it didn't matter to him. But why should it? He didn't go in for things like tradition. "You aren't planning to have a tree?"

"I don't even know where I'll be on Christmas."

"With your family?" She couldn't imagine Christmas without her mother and Hugh.

Could Jason be that detached? Didn't his family celebrate, even with several different mom-and-child combinations?

He still hadn't answered her question.

"Aren't you going home?" She handed him a moist paper towel, but he wasn't entirely covered in glue the way everyone else had been: she and Julia and Anita Kaufman and the rest of the small class who'd agreed to be her guinea pigs.

"Christmas is like Thanksgiving. It's just

a day, Fleming. I don't have children. I don't have to eat cookies for Santa or carrots for Rudolph."

"You have family. Surely you all want to be together." She hated the thought of his loneliness; it seemed so sad to her. Someone ought to do something about it.

"Can we talk about something else?" he asked, though it was clearly not a question.

She didn't want to make things worse for him, but a small voice whispered that he hadn't stayed within the bounds of temporary bank manager. He'd intruded in her life just because he thought he should. Surely she could return the favor. But he'd interfered with her business life. That was different.

"Okay," she said. "We have to go to carol practice, anyway."

"What?" He looked as eager to sing carols with her and her friends as he might be to make another ornament for a tree he didn't plan to put up.

"What if Gabe and Anita see the rest of us practicing on the courthouse steps, and you're not with us?"

He stared at her, not following. "There's really a group?"

She laughed. "They started practicing at Thanksgiving."

He remembered. "You think Gabe and his family are going to search a crowd of carolers for me?"

"I have no idea. But you turned him down for dinner, and when you looked as if you needed help coming up with a reason, you made me your accessory. You have to come sing with us."

"You don't take 'no' easily," Jason's grin told her he didn't see that as a bad thing. He looked doubtful, but not entirely against the idea.

"I can't sing," he warned. "Your group will be sorry if you force me to do this."

"No one is against you here, Jason." She smiled, letting herself feel how much she liked him, but so much emotion startled her enough to make her try to take it back. "Well, hardly anyone."

"Thanks," he said, his wry tone touching her.

"You don't have a choice about this unless you want to hurt your friend's feelings. You should have let him take you to dinner."

"Maybe I should have." Jason gazed at her

as if he couldn't believe she'd caught him in this net. She wasn't sure how she'd done it, either. She wasn't even sure she should have, but she wanted time with him whether getting close to Jason was good for her or really bad.

She excused herself to the back room and changed quickly, wondering whether he'd duck out the door if she took too long and there'd be no decking the halls, after all. To her surprise, when she walked out, hopping to put on one of her ballet flats, she found Jason righting the train cars and tracks that had suffered derailments during the class.

"You like those," she said.

"It was this or pretend I didn't notice all the people walking past the window, staring in and wondering what I'm up to."

She looked outside. Lights flickered green and red and blue from the stars on the streetlamps. "I'll bet they did stare. I didn't think of that. There'll be talk about us in the old town tonight."

Jason glanced at the window again, to find an elderly man peering at him with disapproval as he passed. Fleming laughed. Mr. Fogerty never approved of anyone, but Jason wouldn't know that.

"Apparently so," he said.

"Julia told me people have been suggesting you're offering me special treatment."

"But you know that's not true."

"Not unless you also have a soft spot for Mr. Limber," she said. "I'm not going to worry about what anyone says—let's just enjoy the fun this evening, even if we are hoisting on our own petard."

"How old are you?" he teased, holding the door for her, and then following her through and waiting while she locked it. "My grandfather says that."

"Think what you like. I spent a lot of time with elderly people when I was young," she said. "I was shy, and my mom's older friends liked me. I liked their stories. I didn't know I wasn't cool."

What the heck was wrong with her and her loosened tongue? Something about Jason Macland compelled her to confess her every thought, as if she were under spotlights in a police station.

He didn't need to hear all about her. He already knew too much.

She wouldn't worry about that, either. Tonight was about having a good time. It wasn't a lifetime commitment, and she didn't have to let him get too close.

And that would be easy. He didn't want to be close at all.

## CHAPTER SEVEN

HE DIDN'T RECALL ACTUALLY agreeing to join the carolers, but somehow, there he was. It was dark, and sleet was falling from the night sky when they walked up to the group gathering once more on the piazza in front of the courthouse entrance.

Conversation came to a halt as they approached. Fleming was right about the gossip around here. Jason didn't feel particularly welcome until she got the attention of the crowd, smiling, her hair shining in the lights from the building.

"Everyone, this is Jason Macland. He's going to sing with us." Already he knew her well enough to recognize the pleasure in her tone.

"Really?" That was a man's voice. "I didn't know he was going to stay for Christmas."

"Yeah. Christmas doesn't really seem like his thing," another man said.

Fleming swung around. "Excuse me? Since when are we rude to someone who wants to join our caroling group?"

"Oh," said the second man's voice. "Sorry."

"No problem." Jason had been more insulted in his own home. His dad had believed in toughening up his kids with harsh comments. And then there were the clients who hadn't been thrilled with Jason's advice.

"No, man." The guy came forward, and Jason recognized Denny Harnell, who owned a small restaurant that specialized in hot dogs and different iterations of fries, on the road out of town that led to the resorts on Bliss Peak. "I shouldn't have said anything. You're just doing your job. Same as the rest of us."

"I get it." Jason shook his hand, and Denny pounded his shoulder.

"What are we starting with?" Fleming asked. "'Good King Wenceslas'?"

"Your favorite," said a chorus of voices, as if repeating a familiar chant.

Jason didn't even know the words to the song. He stepped into the group and it seemed natural to end up next to Fleming.

In the cold night air, she let her elbow rub against his. He felt like a teenager, happy because a woman he cared too much for didn't pull away from him.

Not at first, anyway. After a few seconds, she edged far enough away to apply an elbow to his ribs. "You're not singing."

"I am."

She laughed at his lie, and he felt ridiculous. Why was he even here? The singers around them sent them both reproving looks. The good people of Bliss took their caroling seriously. Jason mouthed words, not even close to whatever they were singing, as Fleming belted them out beside him. Shouldn't they have some sort of songbook?

He plunged his hands into the pockets of his wool overcoat. Even if he had printed lyrics, he wouldn't be able to hold them, since his fingers had gone numb.

The longer they stood on the courthouse steps, singing, the larger the crowd they drew. He'd never seen carolers practice before. But their audience began to sing along with them. As soon as they got King Wenceslas back into his castle, someone on the frozen grass below began a thin warble of "White Christmas," and everyone except Jason joined in.

"Even you have to know this one," Fleming said.

He did, but was still reluctant for her to hear his tuneless singing voice. When she nudged him with her elbow again, he finally gave in and sang as close to silently as he could manage. Fleming's grin, and the way she leaned into him, made him feel less foolish.

He stared at her, because he couldn't look away. Even troubled by her business with the store, she could put her problems behind her to join in celebrating the holiday with her friends. He'd never managed to blend the two parts of his life so well.

Business, he understood.

Watching Fleming's changing expression, the way her lovely mouth curved, promising sweetness, he joined in, decking halls and warning about naughty and nice lists and Santa coming to town.

Jason forgot the cold and kept time with the others, singing as if he knew how. Finally, before he realized any time had passed, a guy in front called out that it was late.

"Practice on Friday again." He waved his arm at the singers and then turned to the crowd of onlookers. "Y'all come back on Friday and sing with us, too."

Families broke off from the audience and ambled toward cars or homes. The singers stayed and mingled for a moment. Some agreed to go to dinner, including Fleming, who looked at him, so he guessed he was in for that, too. While Fleming chatted with a man on her other side, Jason turned to the lady on his left.

She turned at the same time, but the smile froze on her face as she recognized him. Amelia Albright, owner of Flowers to the People. She'd missed six payments, and they'd both suffered through an uncomfortable meeting two days ago.

"I wouldn't have pegged you for a singer," she said.

He tried to smile, but his face hurt because business wasn't as satisfying when doing it right hurt a woman. "Nice to see you."

"I'll bet." She folded her hands together and started down the steps.

"Amelia," he said, not certain what he was going to say next. She didn't turn around, but looked back over her shoulder. He had to produce words. What was wrong with him?

"I'm sorry," he said. "I wish I could have done something to make things easier for you."

She said nothing at first. Sleet that had started falling like diamonds from the sky, stung his cheeks. He should have kept his mouth shut.

Amelia glanced at the others, now streaming to their cars. Except for Fleming, who was lurking beside a large, empty planter as if she had urgent business with it.

"I know it's not your fault," Amelia said.

"You didn't have to say that. That isn't why I said I was sorry."

"It's an awkward situation." She shrugged. "I never thought I'd be in a tough spot like this, and it's even harder at the holidays."

As if he'd had the choice of when he came to town and ruined people's dreams. Why hadn't he seen that this would be the worst time?

Even if he had, this was his job. He'd still have had to make the same choices. He couldn't put the bank at risk just to be kind to clients who couldn't make their payments.

He felt as if he was making her situation even worse. "I still wish there were something I could do to help you."

She shook her head as if she couldn't understand him. "See you around." She left, and he didn't think to ask her to stay and have dinner with the rest of the group, not until she was already too far away.

"Are you okay?"

He turned back to Fleming, whose eyes were dark with concern. Her serious expression seemed to thin her face and leave her more fragile.

"I'm fine," he said. He glanced after Amelia Albright. "She's not."

"She's a nice woman. She won't blame you."

"I don't think she does blame me, but that doesn't make it better."

"You're not getting involved, are you?" Fleming asked, and he understood her teasing tone was for his benefit, an effort to ease his guilt.

Before he could answer, the guy who'd suggested dinner named an eatery and told them all to show up in ten minutes.

"We don't have to go," Fleming said.

*We*, she'd said, as if they were together. He wasn't with her. He wasn't with anyone in this town.

"How many people do you think I'm fore-closing on around here?" he asked.

"I think it bothers you to foreclose on any-one."

"You're not wrong. I am human." And he hoped he wouldn't have to foreclose on Amelia. He hated to hurt these people, but the sad, tired truth remained. He had to do his job. "Let's go."

"With everyone else?"

He nodded. Whatever she believed, if it weren't for her, he didn't believe he would have felt so self-conscious about facing the situation. Getting to know her had begun to make everything different.

Names and faces melded for the next few hours. The restaurant was known for its mile-high sandwiches and its groupings of furniture that made the place seem like a series of living rooms. Jason found himself wondering who'd be next in his office at the bank.

But they all treated him as if he was wel-come instead of some psycho mix of the Grinch and Scrooge—which was how he'd begun to feel.

As the evening ended, he spilled out with everyone else, shaking hands and agreeing to attend the Friday practice. Fleming waited for him at the edge of the group.

"You were a better joiner than I was," she said.

He flattened his hand at the back of her waist as they walked toward the square and his hotel. "I enjoyed it. They were friendly, and I like that you're all talking about the future here. They plan to be around."

"We have a nice place to live. I'm not the only one who wants to keep my business."

"You have a nice place and good people." He glanced down the street. "Where's your car?"

"Behind the hotel in the public lot. Why? You want to go somewhere?"

He gazed at her, and the silence around them made the moment more intimate. "No one's ever walked you to your car before?"

She looked at him, startled. A slow, sweet smile curved her mouth. "Dates," she said. "Guys who wanted to go out with me and were trying to make an impression."

Jason laughed. "I thought you knew everyone here. Haven't they already made an impression?"

She glanced at him, her hair framing her

face in soft waves. Her smile remained, shy, tugging at him, warming him.

Warning him. Don't play around with this woman. Don't hurt her by pretending your feet won't itch to move on.

"I was just surprised you would want to come with me," she said, all unaware of the cacophony in his head.

"Even non-dates don't let their friends walk off into the dark." He could have. She was capable. Bliss seemed like a safe place. But as the hour came to end the evening, he didn't want it to end.

"Thanks. I'm happy to have your company."

Her answer surprised him. "Are you afraid of the dark?"

She shoved her hands into her pockets. "I am, a little. Enough that shadows turn into monsters when I least expect it. I once ran from a waving tree limb on Halloween when my friends left me behind while we were trick-or-treating."

"I sometimes wish you weren't so open," he said, smiling to soften the abrupt words.

"I know. I tell you too much. I'm not like that with everyone. You're not, by any chance, afraid of honesty, the way I'm afraid of the dark?"

"I am when it makes me want to protect you." She'd made him frank. Not a great thing. He didn't want to hurt her feelings or make her think there might be more in the future than he had to offer.

"I don't get you. Sometimes you sound as if you've taken a vow to stay away from relationships."

"With people who owe my family's bank money? People whose future is in my hands?"

"I didn't realize banking ethics could be so strict." Her voice was rich with amusement as they turned the corner and left the festive lights on the square behind them. "Do you see all the waving tree branches?"

"Like bony, grabbing fingers." He moved closer to her because he wanted to, even though he knew he shouldn't. "Don't be afraid, Fleming."

Her laughter was a bubble of warmth that seemed to surround them. "If only all fears were as easy to explain away as bony-fingered limbs. Here's my car."

She stepped off the curb. As she touched her door handle, the locks opened. She looked up at him. He'd followed her without thinking, and was standing too close, staring at her pale face, which disturbed him with its sweetness.

"Good night, Jason. You've been a good sport about tonight."

"I had a good time." He wanted to kiss her. Even just to feel the coolness of her cheek against his lips.

"I have to go. Mom's been in town for a couple of days, and I need to see her before she leaves again tomorrow."

He allowed himself to squeeze Fleming's wrist as she held on to the open door. "See you tomorrow."

"Sounds good."

She made the two words sound regretful, as if she, too, wished they didn't have to part.

THE MORNING AFTER the caroling, Katherine was packing to return to Knoxville, where Hugh had begun to grow impatient for her return. Fleming helped her.

"I'm sure we'll be back before Christmas Eve." Katherine tucked her last sweater into the top of her bag. "And if you need me for anything, you can call. Anytime. Ever."

"I'll be fine." Fleming didn't feel fine at all, but having her mother worried and handling her with care only made her more anxious. "I will call if I make a drastic change."

"I've been trying to think of a way to make you believe I want to help."

"I do believe, Mom."

"But you didn't call me when you needed me more than you ever have."

"That was a mistake," Fleming said. "I didn't want to ruin your honeymoon."

Her mother frowned, making an arrow of her brows. "You know I made Hugh wait a long time for me."

Fleming nodded. "I've worried that was because of me."

Her mother shrugged. "Maybe partly, but I wanted the store, too, honey. Maybe I didn't trust Hugh to be the real thing that he is in my life. My one true love. I thought I'd committed to him, but I stayed here, visiting him on weekends, or having him come down. I didn't understand that I had to make the decision to trust him with my life and my future—not until he made me choose to be with him or keep my boundaries up and stay here."

"Why did you marry him if you weren't

sure you could trust him?" Fleming thought of Jason. She didn't want to. He wasn't anything to do with her future. He had no right getting into her head when she and her mother were talking about family.

"I think I saw him as my backup plan. I know now that I had it backward. After I met him, the store should have been my plan B. Hugh should have come first—or first alongside you."

Fleming was bewildered by the concept of holding on to a business in case a marriage didn't work out. But maybe she should be more diligent about making her own just-in-case scenario. She hadn't written a word since her mother had come home. Her backup plan appeared to consist of hiding the fact that she was doing anything except panicking at the thought of losing the store.

"If it comes to the point where we lose Mainly Merry Christmas, it'll be because our best wasn't good enough," Fleming said, as much to herself as to her mother.

"It's your shop now. You don't owe me anything. If it fails or flies, I'm only here to be your soft place to land, not to blame you."

"I want you to go home to your life."

Her mother shook her head. "I see how hard you're working, but I feel as if I should be here beside you."

"No. Did you hear yourself a few minutes ago? Your life is with Hugh now, and this is my choice, to run the store. I'll make it work."

Her mom picked up the suitcase, but doubt strained her expression as she glanced at her watch. "I'd better get going. The traffic around Pigeon Forge can be pretty awful on a Saturday afternoon."

"Let me get your bag." Fleming took it from her mother's hand and carried it down the stairs. She helped her mom stow it in the car and then they walked to the driver's door of her neat little sedan. Katherine pulled her into a quick hug.

"I'm still having second thoughts about leaving."

"The papier-mâché dry run went well, and I'll do everything else we've talked about." They'd discussed a twenty-five days of Christmas promotion that would start on the first of December, along with some new PR on the radio and in the local press, plus on community bulletin boards.

"I'm sure the ornaments will be a success."

"I hope to get out wearing a little less paste next time."

Katherine pulled her close for one last hug as the wind whispered around them. "I love you, honey. Take good care, and remember to enjoy the holidays, too. Don't work yourself to death."

Fleming smiled. She didn't know what else to do, with her mind on the shop, and her concentration focused on not grabbing her mother's arm to take a look at the time on her watch.

Katherine got in the car. Fleming waited until she waved after reversing down the driveway, then ran for her own car and headed into town—to work. Last night had been fun and relaxing, but kind of a break from real life. Today she had to get back to making the business successful.

Normally, Fleming enjoyed the holiday happiness of visitors wandering through the streets in search of the perfect sweater or pancake or hand-tooled leather bag. Today she was beyond driven to open her own door in case someone wanted to come in and buy something.

She grabbed her laptop from the backseat

after she parked behind the hotel. Sometimes she managed to write a few words at lunchtime if the shop wasn't busy. This morning, she needed to do up several varied press releases for the radio. A local cable channel also hosted a bulletin board to boost local business. She'd send something to them, as well.

But first things first.

She hurried through the empty, darkened store, flipping on lights, until she reached the front door. As she opened it, a man passing by glanced up from staring at the sidewalk.

Jason. Moody, serious. A banker.

When he saw her, his eyes softened for the merest second. A slight smile deepened the curve of his mouth. But then he turned his head, exposing a phone at his ear as he looked away.

He kept going. Somehow that hurt. He was busy, not snubbing her. She knew that, but her heightened feelings for him made her sensitive.

She was busy, but if she'd passed him, even while talking on the phone, she would have stopped to say hello.

Because last night had meant something to her, but not to him.

It wasn't his fault. She couldn't be angry. He'd warned her about himself.

For a few hours, he'd seemed like he might think about staying in a sweet, welcoming town full of potential friendships. She'd felt safe in the shadows because she'd been with him, but they couldn't be more than customer and mortgage holder.

She'd do well to follow his lead and stop thinking about him before she got her heart hurt.

Jason was running his business. Sighing, Fleming bent to plug in the train and get back to her own job. She muttered her hopes and prayed that the holiday and the economy would go her way, just long enough to give her shop a firm foundation to stand on into the new year.

Being this afraid made Fleming angry. She had some answers. She just had to take charge and start making the answers work for her. She set up the laptop on the checkout counter and started the first press release before anxiety made her go blank with fear.

MAYBE HE SHOULD have kept Paige around to deal with the actual people who were named in these files, Jason thought. That would have been the easier choice. Staying uninvolved had proved to be impossible. But he'd see that Paige paid for manipulating the bank's customers into the decisions that had gotten them all into this trouble.

It was fine to say that big banks had made bad loans, but in a small town like this, where one man had too much power and too small a heart, things had gotten out of hand in a hurry.

Jason stared at the loan information for Baxter Starnes's family home and literally wanted to be sick. The house had been paid off until Baxter's son developed a mental health issue that had required several years of expensive treatment.

He could see how Paige had convinced the Starnes family they might be able to cover the loan. Barely.

Jason's cell phone vibrated, spinning in a half circle on his borrowed desk. Without looking at the caller's name on the screen, he answered.

"Jason? This is your mother." Her words ran together, almost as if they were one. Jason yanked the phone away from his ear to stare at the screen. How had she gotten his number? "Teresa Macland Brown."

He heard her voice, but it took a second to lift the phone to his ear again. "I know your name."

"I sent you a letter." Her voice broke, her faint hint of nervousness at odds with her brittle tone. "Did you get it? I suppose I shouldn't be surprised that you decided not to respond again."

"Again?" As if she'd been blasting his mailbox with her newsy correspondence for decades. "I got one letter."

"And ignored it. I know I handled leaving badly, but I don't understand why you've always been so determined to make me pay for it for the rest of my life. Haven't you ever made a mistake?"

She made no sense. On the other hand, his family rarely made sense. His father used anger and silence. She'd simply walked away. And somehow they'd tried to make Jason feel as if he was the cause of the problems between him and his parents.

"What is it you want?" He wasn't about to ask what made today different from all the days that had passed since he'd watched her drive off between towering New York City buildings.

"I'm sorry. I'm handling this badly, too. This is not the way I meant to behave. I suppose with your father—"

"I am not my father."

"Maybe I should get to the point before you hang up on me. I've been back in town for several years, and I'm tired of seeing the house in such a state of neglect."

"You live in New York again?"

"Here. In Bliss."

That silenced and shocked him. Did he have a loan in here with his mother's name on it? "My father's bank gave you a mortgage?"

"Not in a million years. He stole my house when he left the marriage."

"He didn't leave."

"I physically left. He was absent long before he dragged us all to New York. At least we had a home here."

"I don't have a clue what you're talking about."

"You might think the past doesn't matter now, but here's what matters. Robert Macland stole my house and everything in it. I chose it. I decorated it. It was my consolation during those years of neglect, and then Robert left my house and everything I cared for to molder."

Jason noticed she didn't say a word about her son. That shouldn't have been a surprise. "You own a house, and my father is keeping you from it?"

"I happen to know it's in your name. I'd like to meet with you to discuss your plans for it."

He laughed, but not with any humor. Teresa Macland Brown appeared to have parted company with reality. "I don't have a house. What's happened to you?" Was she on drugs? Drinking? Delusional?

"Robert put it in your name to keep me from getting it back. Are you pretending you don't know what I'm talking about?"

*He* was arrogant? She brought the word to life. "I don't have a clue whether you believe this story you're telling, but you're wrong. I don't own a house in Bliss, Tennessee. I don't have anything that belongs to you. I haven't even heard from you in two decades."

Her silence, punctuated by short, harsh breaths, screamed frustration. "That's just not true." When she gasped, he froze. From any other woman, it would have sounded like a sob she was trying to silence. "You're my son," she said. "You think I'd leave you to Robert?"

"That's exactly what I know." Her adamancy confused him. "I don't lie," he stated firmly. "If I have a problem with you, I'll tell you, and I have a problem with you calling me now and accusing me of any of this."

She was silent again, but her breathing slowed and calmed. "You really don't know?"

It wouldn't be beyond his father to lie to him, but at this point, Jason had no reason to believe he had.

"I think you should talk to Robert," his mother said. "He's kept you in the dark."

"I'm not—"

"If you aren't going to sell the house, if you decide you want to live in it, I'd like to make a proposition." Her tone went from indignant to pleading. "I could rent the guesthouse from you. I'd be glad to work as caretaker, even if it's in my own home. I can send you references."

She hung up on him. As if he were the one in the wrong. As if he'd abandoned her. And she wasn't his mother.

And all he felt was appalled at her offer to work for him, taking care of a house that apparently he owned, that had belonged to her.

The rage of decades burned through Jason as he curled his hands into fists, trying to hold it all inside. He'd never heard from her after the first few months of her absence, had never had one visit with her. She hadn't called on a graduation day, remembered a birthday, thought of sending even a note on a holiday. The best thing she could do was 'Let me live in my house' because she happened to find out he'd returned to Bliss?

He shoved his phone inside a drawer and tried to get his mind back on his work.

But in the back of his head, all day long, her advice rattled around. *I think you should talk to Robert. He's kept you in the dark.*

Would it be the first time? His father was known for his ability to manipulate businessmen and recalcitrant offspring alike. Most of the decisions Jason had made after college were a response to his refusal to fall in with his father's plans for him.

Robert's favorite method of manipulation had been comparing Jason to his mother, and that had usually bent him to his father's will. So, which parent was lying?

He put it out of his head, compartmentalizing so that the bank's customers didn't suffer for his distracted awareness of just how twisted his family could be.

After the last customer left, smiling for a change because Jason had found a way to extend her loan, he opened his desk drawer and took out his phone.

He dialed his father's private number and got an answer on the first ring.

"What's wrong?" Robert asked.

"My mother called me today. Apparently, she owns a house in Bliss and she thinks I have it."

"Your mother? How did she find you?"

"She lives here. What about this house?"

"Oh. That."

Jason's hand went numb. She hadn't lied. His father would say he hadn't, either. He just hadn't mentioned an ugly truth. Jason had to find a way to ask the right questions if he wanted an answer that included honesty. "What do you mean by 'oh, that'? What did you do to her?"

"After she left me to live with one of my best friends? I made her pay."

He'd never known the guy was a friend of his father's. "I don't care what she did twenty-eight years ago, Dad. How did you make her pay?"

"She thought she could leave me and go back to my hometown. And live in my house, which I bought for her. The house we lived in, there in Bliss. For some reason, she felt she had a right to it. She had no rights after she cheated with my friend. I kept it in the divorce, and then you bought it from me with one dollar of your allowance when you were five."

"I bought it? I don't even remember having an allowance." Jason's memories of the past and his father's descriptions of it rarely matched. "You gave me the house to spite my mother."

"Genetics does not a mother make. Sticking around, showing up. That's what a mother does."

"What about this house?"

"It's yours. The keys are in a safe deposit box in your name there in the bank, along with the title. I've paid the taxes all these years."

"You paid the taxes each year and never told me about it? You were trying to hide what you did."

"You might have given it back to her."

"Apparently I'm enough like you that I won't do that." It didn't make him proud. "What number is the box?" He wanted to see the place. The house that had meant something to both his parents. He had no memory of Bliss, but he had to believe his parents had been happy here once. He wanted to see his home.

"I'll have my assistant send you the information." His father must have turned his chair. The sounds of straining springs and leather were audible in the background. "But don't you give that house back to Teresa."

"Was it hers, Dad?"

"I told you it wasn't. We bought it after we married. She forfeited all right to it when she left. I gave her every penny the court required in the divorce. Do not give her that house. Don't even let her inside. I made sure it belonged only to you."

"And you never told me about it."

"It slipped my mind."

The man was a megalomaniac. This house had been his mother's, just as every home belonged to both husband and wife when a married couple lived there together. "I'll talk to you later, Dad."

"I've been meaning to call you. I owe you an 'atta boy.' You're doing a good job down there."

*Atta boy?* Jason clenched his fist again. "If you'd said that before, Dad, it might have made a difference. But right now, all I can think about is the conversation I just had with my mother."

"Sometimes a man has to do the hard thing, son, for the benefit of the community, or of his children."

"Your children? You mean you kept my mother out of her home for my benefit? I'm not sure how that would work."

"If you think it over, you'll understand. I can tell you know how to make hard decisions from the reports you've been sending us about your work there."

That cooled Jason's temper. He wasn't

comfortable being compared favorably to his father just now. "I'll talk to you later."

He suspected he might have to call his dad and ask for the safe deposit box info again, but just after five an email arrived from Robert's assistant, containing the box number. Jason used the bank's key to open it.

He took the contents out, a long envelope holding legal papers and a set of keys. Aware of sidelong looks from his temporary colleagues, he didn't explain. It was bad enough knowing the truth about his family. Their scandals were his own business.

He tossed the envelope into his briefcase and exited the bank through the back door, meeting no one as he walked down the sidewalk. At the hotel, he went into the dining room, sat at the closest table and ordered coffee.

He opened the long envelope and slid the contents onto the snowy tablecloth in front of him. He unfolded the document and paged through it. It was a deed, stating that he owned a home at 96 Oakwood Drive.

He had no memory of that house. As far as he could remember, he might as well have been born in the penthouse in New York that his mother had left behind.

He picked up the keys, two of them on a leather ring, with a still-shiny gold *M* in the middle of a leather disc.

As the server arrived with his coffee, Jason glanced around the room and discovered he wasn't the only one tucking into caffeine to drown his problems. Fleming, looking worried as she absently spooned sugar into her cup.

She was looking through him as if he wasn't actually there, but when she took a sip of her overly sweet coffee, she grimaced and focused. Seeing him, she blushed as if she were afraid he could read her troubled mind.

He hesitated for a second, not sure he was ready to share his newly discovered secret, but then gathered up the items and his briefcase and went to join her.

"Rough day?" he asked, settling across the table from her.

"Sort of. I'm just worried, about things." Clearly shaking off her anxiety, she took a closer look at the keys and papers. "Don't tell me you took someone's house?"

"Actually, the house seems to be mine," he said, and they were both silent.

He hadn't meant to tell her. He didn't want to talk about it. How could anyone with even the semblance of a normal family understand the way his worked?

Her mother had waited quite a while to marry her new husband, for the sake of Fleming's happiness, apparently. Why hadn't Katherine taken her daughter to live with them, instead of putting her life and her husband's on hold? Remembering his own blended family, Jason could understand her possible reluctance to think her daughter and her new husband would mix.

Whatever her mother's motivation had been, she clearly loved Fleming. Jason's mom had driven away and barely ever looked back. His father believed in ruling by the most spectacular unkindness.

"Wait. Are you saying you didn't know you owned a house here in town?" Fleming asked.

He shook his head. It sounded ludicrous to him, too.

"So you've never seen it?"

Again he shook his head, but then noticed her curious expression. "I'm on my way to look for it now." He scooped up the papers and keys. "Do you know where Oakwood Drive is?"

"Yes."

"Do you want to show me the way?"

She measured him with her gaze as if she wasn't sure he was serious. "Heck, yeah." She grabbed her purse and stood. "Let's go. I can't imagine suddenly discovering you own a house."

She weaved through the tables to the hotel's entrance hall, where she paused, her slender fingers flexed against the wood of the heavy door. She had such graceful hands. "You don't, by chance, owe a mortgage on that place?"

He grinned. "That I haven't been paying? No, but I'm happy to offer you a moment of joy at the thought of my misery."

Her laughter made him want to put his hands on her shoulders and pull her closer. He craved her easy warmth, the kindness in the way she forgot her own troubles long enough to be concerned about his.

"I didn't mean it that way, but I did, for just a second, sort of hope you might be forced to give everyone a break if you were losing your family's home." She pushed through the door. "How does a person have a family home they don't even know about?"

"You start with a family that defines *dys-functional*."

## CHAPTER EIGHT

FLEMING DIDN'T KNOW what to say as they walked down the sidewalk and around the hotel to his car, parked in a white-pebbled lot. How dysfunctional could one family be?

"I am curious about this place. Apparently Dad just closed it up with everything still inside," Jason said. "But I never knew what I was missing because I didn't know about the house until today."

The car lights flashed and the doors unlocked automatically as Jason reached the driver's side. Fleming opened the passenger door, flummoxed by his situation.

"I can't believe no one in your family ever mentioned it."

"We're not really a sharing kind of family. My mother hardly spoke to me after the day she left, and my dad keeps his personal business…well, personal. It's a power thing. I try to stay in touch with my brother and two sisters, but they only respond if they're on the outs with my dad."

"I don't understand. You have a dad and a brother and sisters? And a mother? And you've never mentioned any of them? Even when I told you about my father?"

"I do, Fleming, but I wasn't about to try to top your story with my own. You're not an amateur psychologist, are you?"

His gentle teasing embarrassed her. "Just inappropriately curious," she said with a rueful grin. "And when you say you're not in touch, do you mean that you really don't speak to each other—very often?" She added the last because the question sounded harsher than she meant to be.

Jason took a deep breath. "Look. My family isn't like everyone else's. I can't explain."

He didn't want to try. Fleming got that loud and clear. She turned her face to the window, not laughing any longer. What right did she have to drill to the bottom of his soul?

"The leaves are mostly off the trees now," she said, changing the subject, tritely grabbing at the first thing in her head. "I think it might snow again."

"I thought this was the South. What's with all the sleet and snow?"

"We're Southerners who live at higher elevations. What makes you so grumpy about it? You come from New York. Besides, you're not staying." She touched his fine wool sleeve. "And while you're here, you have a nice coat. You won't have any trouble staying warm."

"Sorry." He glanced her way with a gentle, apologetic smile. "I'm not complaining. It's just been a strange day."

Her pulse ratcheted up. They might have been any couple, arguing a little and making up on a drive they wanted to share. "I understand the power of a bad day."

They climbed farther up the mountain on roads that twisted back on themselves.

"I know where Oakwood is." Fleming kept an eye out for an old soda advertisement. "There's a big rusted sign that was on the side of a barn at the corner where it meets this road, but sometime while I was in high school the barn fell down. Mr. Potter, who owned the barn, posted it on a fence to show where to turn."

"Do you remember the house my parents owned?"

"No. I rode my bike up here when I was a kid, but I don't think I knew anyone down your road."

"My road," he said, with a sense of surprise.

"I think we're getting close." She pointed to a collection of old boards barely clinging to a gray wooden frame, and a mostly missing, rusted tin roof. "I remember that old chicken house."

"Chicken house? That's a relief. I thought it was someone's shack."

"Very funny. Like no one up here has ever heard jokes like that. The Frosts used to keep chickens here and sell their eggs at the market on the square, but the market's only open now for a few weekends in the summer. In the winter, they hook up with some sort of organic delivery service, and they built a bigger house closer to town a few years ago. Do you remember a family named Frost?"

"I don't remember anything."

"How old were you when your family left Bliss?"

"Too young to remember ever being here."

The edge in his voice touched her, but she had no idea what to say to make it better.

"See that sign?" Hanging by one side now. Someone had been using it for target practice. "Turn left there."

"Thanks."

"What do you think you'll do with the house?" He wouldn't be staying in it. He didn't have to remind her of that.

"I don't have a clue. It's probably a mess. Who knows? It might even be condemned by now. I just want to see it."

Would he remember anything? What was it like going back to a past that was a total mystery? "So you don't think your family— your father—maintained it?"

"I'm positive he didn't. He paid the taxes, but only gave it to me to keep it away from my mother."

"He did what?" Even her father hadn't taken active steps to leave them destitute— other than abandoning them.

"My mother left my father, and he held a grudge."

"You say that so calmly, but he punished you both. He didn't tell you about the home, and he somehow knew your mother wouldn't, either." Jason's stillness was a palpable force that energized the car, like lightning building up to strike. "None of which is my business," Fleming said.

"I know what you mean. They were unkind to each other."

His voice had deepened.

"I just can't believe she never tried to contact you." It was hard to grasp. Fleming's own mother would never have let her go like that.

"She was busy with her own life. I'm wondering now if my dad made it hard for her to see me. After a while I stopped hoping she'd come."

"I'm sorry, but I don't believe that. I never stopped wishing my dad would come back, and every time he said he would come see me, I believed him—or at least I hoped he'd finally show up."

Jason's quick glance was concerned enough to make her feel his warmth.

"Have you ever asked your father what went wrong?" Fleming murmured.

"I never had to. My mother told him she loved someone else, and believe me, I remember that scene between them. I begged her to stay while she packed, but she wouldn't even speak to me. Later, I watched her drive away with the other guy. Her actions spoke louder than any words."

Fleming couldn't find words to fill the terrible silence. She hurt for him.

"I owe you for coming with me, Fleming."

"No. I should tend to my own problems and stay out of yours. I don't want you to see this place on your own. No one should have to deal with such a strange thing alone, finding you own a house that was used as a weapon. But I'm curious, too."

Her family seemed straightforward when she compared her childhood to Jason's. No secrets. Just horrible regret.

Jason's past seemed to be a closed book that no one ever opened. He hadn't been allowed answers. What was odd to her was that he'd just acquiesced with the silence.

The car's atmosphere seemed to thicken, just like the trees around them. No businesses and few homes had ever thinned out this forest. But the narrow roads remained to hint at settlers who'd made this climb back when the land was new and farming demanded larger properties.

"I can't read that street sign ahead," she said, realizing the sky was growing darker.

"I can't believe the county even bothers with signs up here."

"Maybe they knew your father better than you did. They guessed someone would finally come home."

Jason grinned at her and pressed a quick, capable hand to hers, making her breathing constrict. "That's a hopeful thought. Not sure it's worth thinking, though. Maybe one of my sisters or my brother will want it. My grandparents owned a place here somewhere, too. They sold it when they moved to New York with us."

"I wonder why I didn't know about any of this. I'm a country kid. I've run over these mountains and played in these fields. Abandoned homes were like clubhouses to us."

"Us?"

"My friends and me when we were growing up. This is a town without a lot of future unless the tourism industry inspires you. People move out. Families lose their homes, or they try to sell, until they realize they can't, but they have to live elsewhere."

"So other troubled families left, too. Sounds pretty bleak." He peered through the windshield at a forest gone wild. "Maybe that's why no one talked about us."

"Yeah. It would have been like borrowing bad karma." She leaned her head against the side window, peering out. "I'm guessing we'll find a driveway. Maybe a mailbox post."

"Good enough. We'll search all the abandoned driveways we come across."

They had to search only one. After several feet, they reached cracked concrete with brown weeds growing up through the breaks in it. At the top of the drive they found a two-story blue house.

"That doesn't look so bad. The paint's in good shape," Fleming observed. Only a few of the shutters were hanging. "That's a huge garage."

"This must be it. My dad always had several cars he was restoring."

She was surprised. "Odd hobby for the guy you describe."

"Because he had to get his hands dirty?" Jason eased over a crevice in the driveway. "That's the only time he gets them in the dirt and oil."

A broken parking area out front offered just enough room for the SUV.

Fleming opened her car door and got out. Up close, the house's flaws were easier to see. The place looked haunted—not a home at all. Its emptiness was a low howl in the cold, windy silence.

Only the garage looked as if it could be habitable. Jason's father had kept that up at some point, with more care than he'd given his home.

She went around the car, compelled by an urge to protect Jason from all this neglect, But just in time, she remembered they didn't have that kind of relationship, and she had no right.

She stopped before she reached him. "How long since anyone's lived in it?"

Jason's face was expressionless. He'd perfected hiding his emotions. He stared at the peeling paint, the wooden porch with railings missing, the shattered windows framed by filthy shutters. "I'm not sure. I don't know if my father rented it out. I couldn't find anything in the records, and I won't be asking him."

"Wow." There didn't seem to be a lot more to say. That she felt sorry for him, he wouldn't welcome. That she was appalled his father would let the house fall into disrepair, he probably didn't want to hear again.

But she hoped he hadn't suffered the same neglect this house had endured, living with a man who could walk away from so much.

"I get that he didn't want to live in it, and he didn't want my mom to have it," Jason said. "But why let it fall into ruin?"

Fleming couldn't tell if he was expecting an answer. He might not even know he'd spoken aloud. "Maybe he was trying to forget something that happened here?" she ventured.

"It's not like he killed my mother and buried her body on the property. I don't know what he'd want to forget." Jason headed toward the stairs. "At first I thought they must have been happy here because they lived in this house at the beginning of their marriage. Now I wonder if they ever knew happiness."

"Where is your mom now?" Fleming asked, curious enough to take advantage of a possible moment of weakness.

"Somewhere in town here." He turned his head, his face bleak and yet still blank. "She called me today."

"What? Your mother lives here? Do I know her?"

"I have no idea. Her last name is Brown now. Maybe she never uses Macland."

This man kept secrets as well as his father did. That fact seemed relevant to every conversation they'd had. "That's how you found out about the house? She told you in the phone call? I thought you hadn't heard from her."

"I haven't until today. I was surprised when she called. She'd sent a letter a few days ago."

"With no address?"

"No. Just mine, and a request that I see her."

Fleming was startled again, as more of this story unfolded, piece by piece. "You didn't think that was odd?"

He looked back at her. "She seems to think this is all some choice I made."

"I didn't mean that." Fleming knew what it was to be a child in the middle of angry, divorced parents. "But why don't any of your family ask questions of each other?"

"You can ask all you want, but sometimes you can't pry the answers out of someone who doesn't want to talk."

"You've got that right. Did you ask your mother where she is in Bliss?"

Shaking his head, he started for the house

again. "She didn't volunteer her address, and I didn't ask. Normally, it's the child who runs away. Not in my family."

"Maybe she was hoping for acceptance."

He looked irritated. Fleming couldn't blame him.

He turned toward the blue house. "You weren't in on the phone call. Did you manage to accept your father after he left?"

She shook her head, even though Jason couldn't see, and the cold mountain air kissed her cheek. "He died before I ever found a way to trust him again, and I feel bad about it."

Jason went to reach for her, but he must have drawn the same conclusion she had about comforting him. His hand froze in midair.

They stared at each other in a silence broken only by the rustle of dry leaves and the whistle of wind through broken windows.

His expression finally softened. He smiled at her with a look that asked her to understand him. "I'm sorry about your father."

"So am I." The blood seemed to rush in her ears. She never talked about him, not even with her mother.

"But I can't just pretend nothing happened

with my mom," Jason continued. "She left, and she never made any effort to see me or even talk with me. She's only getting in touch now because she wants this house."

"What if it's an excuse for her to contact you? After you showed up in town? Could be that after all these years, she didn't know how to do it, so she thought of this."

From the way he grimaced, suggesting his mother's behavior was an error in the woman's judgment might be like grinding salt into a raw wound.

"Like I said before, you weren't in on the call."

"But what if you change your mind, only to find you're too late? Maybe that's exactly the reason we should try to accept people. Being bitter did me no good, and it certainly brought me no feeling of relief. My dad finally came back and asked me to make things right, but I couldn't. And then—well, I just waited too long." She covered her mouth with her fingertips. She'd told him too much. She didn't want his sympathy, and her own wound was pretty raw, too.

"Forgiveness would be good for me?" He walked toward the house again. "I should have asked my mother to meet me here. If she saw this place, she'd probably betray her true colors. The house is likely too derelict to be repaired."

"You can't know for sure that she's trying to manipulate you. I mean, she obviously never explained to you what she was thinking, but a parent must have a reason to run away from her own son."

He turned back. "What was your father's reason for staying away from you?"

Fleming stopped as if he'd slapped her.

"My dad never gave me a reason. He'd promise he was coming for me on a specific day at a specific time, and I'd be like one of those kids in a movie about broken families—sitting on the curb with my tiny suitcase packed. Truly heartbroken with disappointment when he didn't turn up. Over and over. And I refused to go inside. As if waiting was some sort of cosmic way to pull him to me. I was hard to convince, but finally, I had the choice of either crying my eyes out until I was old enough to tell him to stop making me believe he cared about me, or I could assume he wasn't going to come."

"But you said he finally did show up?"

Jason went up the front wooden steps, testing each one for safety.

"He did, sometimes. I learned to pack in a hurry if he actually arrived. My mom was never that thrilled to see him, and when Hugh came along, he acted the way he has ever since—as if he was protecting his own child. I can count on him."

"I never had that," Jason said. "But at least my mother never promised she was going to visit."

"Maybe it's better that way. I can't adequately express how that kick in the gut hurt. Every time."

Jason held out his hand. Fleming stared at his broad palm, tempted because no matter how many times she'd been abandoned, she couldn't quite believe she wasn't lovable.

She put her hand in Jason's.

He tugged her over a particularly weak board, and she laughed to hide her embarrassment. She was still so gullible, so eager. He'd offered his hand only to help her up the rickety stairs. No doubt he was seeking to avoid a lawsuit if the place fell in.

"It's the House of Usher," she said, and

grinned up at him. "The story by Poe, not the home of the singer."

"No explanation needed."

"Sorry. I make jokes when I'm feeling awkward."

He tried another couple stairs. "You should put your feet exactly where I've put mine."

"I'm not sure it's best to strain the boards in the same place more than once."

He laughed. After reaching the porch, he crossed to the door, which swung inward the second he touched it. It gave a prolonged creak that sounded like a ghostly scream in one of those half comedy, half horror movies where terrible things happened, but with lots of bad jokes.

Fleming pointed at the hole in the door where a knob had been. "Someone stole it."

"If it was period, it was probably valuable. I doubt anything's left if it's this easy to get inside." He stepped over the threshold.

From behind him, she peered around his shoulder. Plaster was peeling off the walls and ceilings. There were so many holes it looked as if trespassers just hadn't liked using the wide doorways.

"And someone took the light fixtures, too," she said.

"They were probably also period," he said. "I was able to search the tax records, and the house was built in the late 1800s."

"I don't understand how everyone left." She glanced at his set jaw. "Your whole family, I mean."

"My father was an only child. He met my mom in college. His parents lived here, but they came to New York to look after me. Otherwise, I'd have been in the care of nannies, and my grandparents didn't want that, though I don't imagine either of my folks would have minded."

"Then your father remarried?"

"My sisters have one mother and my brother has another. We had no continuity. My dad was busy, busier as I got older. Their mothers were more in their lives than mine was, but our grandparents were the constant. They are the constant for all of us." He went farther inside.

"Jason, you should be careful. This floor can't be safe."

He bounced a little on his toes. The wide

planks held. "It feels steady. Wait here. I just want to look around."

"You mean wait by myself?"

"In case you're right about the floor."

Surely the weather was too cold for snakes. But not for squatters or snoopy people like her. "Don't go. This place is creepy."

"Are you afraid?" He smiled as if the thought amused him, but kept going. "I won't be long. I just want to see what's left."

She started to follow, but hesitated, uncertain of protocol. "Do you want privacy?"

"For what?"

"Your memories? I like to be alone with mine when they're…" She almost said *painful*, but she'd shared enough personal stuff for one day. She'd never had memories like the ones that must be dying inside this house. "…intense."

"I have no memories of this home. It isn't going to hurt."

There wasn't even a picture left. Someone had stolen all the furniture except for broken sticks here and there that might once have belonged to chairs or tables. An old chintz cushion was wedged beneath the living room window. If anyone had ever been happy here, no one would be able to remember in all this musty gloom.

Any aid to memory had been stolen or thrown away.

"It was your home, though, once. If things had been different, it might still be," she mused.

"Don't get carried away," Jason said. "I don't need a home here after I finish my work at the bank. If I needed convincing about that, this is it."

"Oh." She'd thought finding a home he could make his own might feel like a new beginning to him, but he somehow thought it underscored the ending.

Just in case she needed a reminder of how he looked at his world.

## CHAPTER NINE

JASON FELT AS if he should hold on to Fleming as they investigated the main floor. The fireplace in the living room was missing bricks. Many of the windows were open to the cold air. She was right about the floors. They did feel suspiciously bouncy.

"Careful," he said. "We probably shouldn't be in here." Or she shouldn't. Why had he thought bringing her would be a good idea?

He hadn't wanted to be alone, coming to a place that might evoke memories. And yet if he were a less pragmatic man, he might believe the house was a victim of the bitterness that made his father resent his first wife so much he was still keeping the house from her. And his mom was clearly still furious with Robert.

"I want to see it all. I'm stunned that it's sat here empty all these years," Fleming was saying.

"It's likely my father forgot about it."

"He can't have been that determined to keep it out of your mother's hands."

She said it so matter-of-factly. "That doesn't seem believable to you?" he asked.

She shrugged, skidded on a piece of wallpaper lying loose on the floor, and caught his arm. "It seems like a ridiculous waste of time and emotional energy."

"Emotional energy?" he asked.

"You know—wasting all your feelings on something you can't change. Even two decades later."

"I don't think he wants to change it. He wants her to be unhappy. The guy she left with was his best friend."

Jason said that as if it wasn't surprising. He was wishing he'd kept it to himself when Fleming's silence made him glance down at her.

"What?" he asked, trying to understand her troubled expression.

"Could you want vengeance that long?"

He sincerely hoped he wouldn't ever waste that much of his life. "I don't intend to put myself in that position."

Her smile was more of a grimace. "I forgot. You're planning to remain distant from all human communication."

"You're really an understanding woman." He stepped away from her, through an arching doorway, and found himself in the remains of a kitchen. "Don't ever let anyone tell you that you don't have a big heart."

"Sorry." She crossed to the counter beneath the window, completely ignoring the wooden floor groaning beneath her feet. "Someone made away with your sink." She peered into the open hole. "And they used the cabinet as a garbage can. Someone really enjoys Mc-Donald's."

"Let's go before you fall through to the basement and sue me for the cost of your mortgage," he said.

"I'm fine. How many bedrooms do you think this place has?"

"Are you in the market?" He wasn't fine. He didn't want to discuss his abandoned home. He'd prefer not to confide any more of his family's scandals, and he didn't want to feel any closer to Fleming Harris.

"I'm thinking of you. You'll need to either knock it down or put it back together."

"Why do I have to do anything with it at all?"

She went to the wall of windows at the back of the kitchen. "They must have put a table here in the old days." She peered through the dirty glass—what was left of it. "Come look. It's beautiful."

He joined her. At the end of a sloping lawn, the Smokies rolled away into the distance. Ridge after ridge, covered in brown hardwoods and verdant evergreens spun a soft painting. Mist-and-snow-dotted peaks that seemed to be shaded in soft blue.

Winter was taking over the landscape. It should have looked cold, but it was so beautiful it tugged at him. This view had been his once. And his father's and mother's when they'd been a family. The family he couldn't remember.

"What do you think?" Fleming asked, as if she were selling him that view.

"It's nice, but it's not really mine."

"Why couldn't it be?"

"Why not raze it?" Jason asked, knowing he would never do that. "I don't have time to spend in the mountains, an hour and a half from the nearest airport."

"You can land a helicopter here, and this could be a vacation home. And don't you ever work from home? Isn't that the advantage of consulting?"

"Why are you thinking all this over, Fleming?"

She blushed. "I'm thinking this is an amazing spot, and it's a beautiful house still. It's just a little broken."

Like him? Was she implying he was like this house? Ridiculous. One conversation with each of his parents, and he'd turned paranoid.

"Let's go." But instead of taking her hand and dragging her out of the derelict building, he was drawn back to the mountains outside that broken window.

It had been a home, and he didn't have to repeat his parents' mistakes. It was a place his sisters and brother might come to. His grandparents spoke of Bliss with a longing that made him feel guilty, because he was the reason they'd given up their life here.

But it didn't make sense. He'd been born here, but it was no part of his real life.

He turned toward the archway that led

to the next room. "Come on, Fleming. We should get out of here before it gets too dark."

"Wait. Can't we go upstairs?"

"You sound like a kid, asking permission," he said, and wished it was easier to say no to her.

"It's your house, and I may never be invited back. I'd like to see the upstairs."

He ignored her uncomfortable suggestion. "Until the stairs start to creak."

She hurried ahead of him, cute and excited and happier than he knew how to be, over an old house that had too much past and no future.

"Can't you slow down?" he asked, as she hurried up the first three stairs.

"No, because you'll change your mind and call me back." She glanced around as she reached the landing. "Wow. You have to see this."

"What is it?" He followed her. She'd stopped, and he peered up the stairs beyond her. The light coming through the huge circular window in front of them was turning a darker blue-gray with every minute. "I can't see up there."

"This." She opened her hands to show him

the landing, as wide and spacious as a small room in any other house. "Wouldn't it be perfect with chairs and a table? You could read here or write." She stared at him. "Letters, I mean. Something like that. Homework, if you were a kid."

Her enthusiasm was like a new coat of paint and some sturdy joists beneath their feet. She saw possibilities despite the neglect. He saw only the anger that had caused it. He could use a change of scenery.

"Maybe you should make me an offer," he said, and then rushed to clarify. "On the house."

BY THE TIME Jason parked in front of Mainly Merry Christmas, it was dark, and Fleming had rebuilt the house in her head. She was glad they'd gotten beyond her suggestion to make it a vacation house. A guy like Jason didn't need a summer place like his forgotten home in the Smokies.

He probably saw success as a mansion in the Hamptons or a villa somewhere in the Mediterranean, all completely outside the sphere of her imagination. She felt like an idiot. She had to focus on her store, not on his future.

"Thanks for letting me go along," she said, reaching for the door handle.

"Thanks for coming."

"I think I may have gotten overly excited about your place up there. You can tell I like to make things cozy." She pointed at the store. "Every day is a lead-up to the holidays in my life."

"Don't worry about it," he said. "I don't mind talking."

She smiled at him because he was lying. She was positive that every personal admission from him came at a price.

The car was feeling far too snug now, with the silence broken and his frustration liable to return at any moment. "I'll see you at caroling practice," Fleming said.

He nodded. "If I can make it."

Great. He was so wary of being involved, he was pulling away from that, as well. "Good night."

She climbed out of the car and went into the store without turning. Only lovesick schoolgirls looked back to see if the object of their fantasies was watching them walk away.

She seriously wanted to know, but she didn't let herself check. She had to get her mind on her own business again and stay out of Jason's. If he didn't feel the same ready attachment she found toward his beautiful, neglected home, she couldn't make him feel it.

She shouldn't keep trying.

Turning over a more businesslike leaf, she set up stations for making the papier-mâché ornaments. One of the local schools was bringing in their second graders on a field trip the next day.

A few customers came in for cards and tinsel and lights, and to inquire about the special ornaments she and her mother ordered each year for the store. Fleming had put in this year's order late, but they were due to arrive within the week.

At just after nine, she turned down the store lights so that the Christmas lights furnished a twinkling, joyous background as she opened her laptop on the counter. She promised herself she'd stay for only an hour to write a quick scene.

She had to be up early in the morning to start the workday over again.

She read through the last couple pages

she'd written and then dived in. Time slipped past her. Swimming in the world inside her story, she noticed nothing outside it until a sound at the front of the store dragged her back to reality.

She looked up, feeling a little as if she were waking from a dream. A woman stood outside the plate glass window, tall, too slender, wearing an aqua uniform that Fleming recognized from one of the resorts up on the mountain.

The woman stared at the window display with a look of great sadness. For reasons she couldn't explain, the hairs on the back of Fleming's neck stood up, but she didn't move. She didn't blink.

After several unnerving seconds, the woman smiled, sadly, but sweetly, and looped her dark, wavy hair behind her ears. She wrapped her arms around her waist.

"Oh," Fleming said out loud. Her unusual visitor wasn't even wearing a coat.

She quickly saved her work and shut her laptop, but by the time she went to the front door, the woman had gone. Fleming opened the door and looked down the street, just in time to see the aqua uniform, glowing in moonlight, disappear into the nearest alley.

What to do? Should she call police? The woman might need help. But she seemed to have a job. That didn't mean she was all right. That missing coat was worrisome.

Why had she been so interested in the store?

Fleming backed up and looked inside. All she could see was the counter where she'd been standing, and all the blinking lights making shadows of the trees and shelves.

Maybe the woman had been lonely. Or wanted to buy something she couldn't afford. Fleming glanced toward the alley, wishing she could have caught her in time to offer her coffee or cocoa—or a cup of soup.

She shuddered all the same as she went back inside and turned the lock on the door. She might be worried about the woman, but the moment had been creepy.

THE MORNING AFTER he'd visited the house, Jason woke late and rolled out of bed. He opened his door to grab the newspaper Lyle Benjamin, the landlord, left daily in the hall.

It was there, but on top of it was a toy, a

box containing a purple action figure, the villain in a kid's animated show from back when Jason was a child. He stared at it, perplexed, and then glanced up and down the hall.

Still in its mint-condition packaging, the toy didn't seem like a mistake, like something another guest's child might have tired of and then set on top of Jason's paper as he passed by.

He picked up the toy and the paper and went back into his room, turning the cardboard with its plastic-wrapped action figure over in his hand. He'd wanted one of these once, about a billion years ago.

His father had believed in a different kind of toy, something educational, or a book. A computer that had made Jason a hero among his friends, whose parents hadn't believed them mature or responsible enough to have one.

Behind him, an antique clock chimed the hour from the mantelpiece, with a froufrou, girlie affectation that annoyed him every time it reminded him he was running late.

Something about this town was changing him. He never ran late for appointments.

He rushed through a shower and grabbed

the toy on his way out of his room. Down-stairs, he cornered Lyle, who was just bring-ing in firewood.

"I think some kid left this at my door by mistake." Jason set the purple villain on the reception desk. What little boy carried around an unopened, newly bought, vintage toy?

Lyle glanced at it. "That doesn't seem likely. I don't think you can find these in stores anymore. I have a nephew your age, and he collects those."

Jason didn't know whether to laugh or pay attention to the pain that seemed to clench in his rib cage. If someone had meant this for him, he could imagine only one person bring-ing the toy to the hotel and then not staying to hand it to him.

He pretended to feel nothing. "You're not suggesting it's your grown nephew's, and it got delivered to my room by mistake?"

"I'm saying it couldn't have gotten to your room by accident. They're not that easy to find, and they're expensive when they're mint, in the box."

Jason stared at it. His mother. Had she still been around when he'd wanted this guy? When this toy had been the one that would have made him the happiest little about-to-be abandoned kid ever? How would she have found it?

It was a crazy thought, but it had to have been she who dropped this off for him. She had to have a motive, a plan. Was she asking him to remember the past? Was she asking for forgiveness?

His anger suddenly dissipated like air released from a balloon. Maybe he had no right to judge, or to withhold forgiveness. He wasn't a child anymore, a fact that might have escaped him until he held this toy, the object of his toddlerhood's delight, in his hands.

His mother had known him. She had remembered. Even if she was just reiterating that she wanted the house, she'd done it with something that had mattered deeply to him back then.

Maybe Fleming hadn't been completely wrong. She regretted holding a grudge against her father. Jason didn't have to knock down the walls and invite his mother into his life, but maybe he could ease the door open and see what she really wanted.

He went to work, but the whole day—discussing loans with residents of Bliss who'd gotten behind in payments, talking to prospective new customers whom he needed to vet before he agreed the bank could give away more of its money—he was aware of snow floating in flurries outside his gothic office window. And of his mother's cell phone number pulsing in the back of his head, unintentionally memorized.

By evening, when he walked out of the building, he was still uncertain about calling.

She'd left the toy at his doorstep. Possibly an effort to manipulate him—if she was the woman his father had described all Jason's life. She wanted her house back. Maybe she didn't think her son had a right to the home he didn't remember. Maybe he didn't.

And what had that hint of hers meant? That his father might have kept her away? That didn't seem so unlikely.

Jason had been his dad's weapon against his mom, but maybe she wanted to use him against Robert now.

But he'd learned young about snap decisions. From the day his mother had left. Snap decisions were never wise, and they'd almost always proved a source of regret to him.

He stopped at the coffee shop for a cup

of their strongest brew and a sandwich of dry turkey on slightly stale bread. Seated at the counter along the window, he set down a sandwich half while he tried to chew.

"Their coffee is great," said a voice behind him.

A voice he recognized because it haunted him. Since the moment she'd refused to leave him when an attacker sailed past her in his office.

"I'd be careful of the sandwiches, though," she said, from closer now. "Technically, they're fresh enough to sell, but they keep them overnight in a fridge. I've never been able to abide a sandwich from the fridge. Which is odd, because all the ingredients come from there. They just don't taste as good when you take them out and put them together."

"It's the bread," he said. "I've never liked bread from a fridge, either."

She laughed. "Something in common. So, are you coming to caroling practice tonight?"

He glanced through the window, plate glass, oddly clean even though trucks had been splashing salt and chemicals all over the sidewalks every time the forecast included a hint of snow. "I may be busy," he said.

She was silent a moment. "Okay."

"Why does it matter to you?"

"You're part of the group," she said. After another few seconds, she nodded. "Except something about seeing your house and hanging out with me has put you out of sorts. You need your distance again."

"You're right. I've gotten myself more involved in this community than I meant to be. I like having someone to eat with. I was glad you came along to that house with me. I like caroling, because no one cares how badly I sing."

"No one can tell who's singing badly because we all sing heinously," she said, but she couldn't hide a small smile that made him feel guilty. He didn't want her to think the house or enjoying the company of her and her friends made a difference to his plans.

"But I think my mother reminded me of my priorities."

"Okay." Fleming's face fell. She looked confused.

He opened his briefcase to show her the toy. "See this?"

"A purple toy skeleton. That's a funny thing to carry to work."

"Did you watch TV when you were a kid?"

"Not much. Mom didn't approve." She stared at the figure. "I read a lot."

"Probably a better choice." They couldn't get through any conversation without learning more about each other, no matter how much he preferred their friendship remain on a surface level. "I wanted it when I was little. There was a time when only this guy would have made my Christmas perfect."

She grinned, but slowly, as if still trying to piece the puzzle together. "Your family had so much money—you lived in a fancy apartment in New York. Your father couldn't find one of those? He couldn't have contacted the manufacturer and snapped one up for you?"

"We didn't live like that."

"He signed a house over to you when you were a toddler, but you lived like the common folk?"

"Don't do this, Fleming. What makes you think I'm some rich guy, pretending not to be?"

"I didn't mean that. But a banker's son, and a business consultant whose career is soaring, piling success on top of success? You could have had a plastic toy anytime you put effort into finding it."

"He didn't think I needed one, and my mother didn't argue. She finally found the courage to give me something my dad didn't want me to have. She's trying to manipulate me by reminding me of the past."

Fleming glanced down at the purple toy illuminated by the stream of light from above the coffee shop counter. "She knows you grew up with your father, but she thinks she can buy you with that?" Fleming picked up his cup as if they were much closer than overly attracted acquaintances. She took a sip of the black coffee and made a face at its bitterness. "She's counting on the idea that you might have changed."

"You know how you said you regretted not giving your father a second chance?" Jason asked.

Fleming made another face, as if she'd overdosed on something more bitter than his coffee. "I gave him about a million chances. At least a million, but I am sorry I didn't give him one last one."

"That makes sense to me." Jason took a

bite of the other half of his sandwich. Most of the bread was still dry, but someone had slopped on some sort of sauce in the middle that made it soggy. He pushed the square white plate away.

"Are you sure she sent that? Did she include a note? What do you think she was trying to say? Give me my house, and I'll give you your toy? "

"That she's still my mother, and that she remembers when I was her son."

"But she has to know there's more to mothering than showing up decades later. I'm surprised."

"Because?"

"Why now? She's either really sorry about the past, in which case you'd think she would have tried to get in touch before now, or she's horribly cruel, trying to manipulate you with a memory that matters so much to you." Fleming picked up a package of crackers and crumbled them, as if she didn't realize what she was doing. "I don't like that idea." She looked up, meeting his gaze with intensity. "I want you to be careful."

He shut the briefcase. "You always surprise

me, Fleming. I thought you'd say I should go for meeting her."

She shut her mouth. "I might have before this, but she knew what you wanted the last time you saw her, and she brought it. That makes me nervous." Fleming ducked her head. "For you. Because I wouldn't want you to be hurt. I hope that doesn't overstep any boundaries."

He shook his head. "I asked what you thought. I appreciate your opinion. It turns out that the real question I want to ask is whether you'd agree to see her if you were in the same situation."

Fleming looked up again. He could tell she was thinking, by the little frown wrinkling the skin just above her nose. "I guess I'd see my father. I'm still sorry I didn't that one last time."

"And if he'd left you hanging that one last time?"

"I wouldn't feel guilty, as if I hadn't done the best I could do. It wasn't my responsibility. That's what my mom told me. I wasn't the adult, but I was close to adulthood by then, and I knew right from wrong. I was just tired of feeling like an idiot for always waiting for him."

"I am an adult." And his mother… The toy. The strange note and call. She seemed troubled. Jason couldn't manage to say that out loud because then he'd be committed.

"You'll do the right thing," Fleming said. "I believe that about you."

Her certainty didn't make him feel better. It made him feel responsible. He found he didn't want to disappoint this woman he hardly knew. "Why do you trust me?" he asked.

Her grin engaged him. He liked the curve of her mouth, the warmth she shared without thinking about what she could gain or lose.

"I didn't say I trusted you." Her tone teased. "I said you'd do the right thing. Look at how you're handling this loan debacle. You may not enjoy coming to town and cutting Christmas to shreds for who knows how many people. But you're doing it. Because you have to."

Because it was the right thing. And she was correct. He hated it.

He'd have been wiser to stay objective. He'd managed it before. Why was Bliss different than all the other towns and cities he'd visited, where he'd had to handle uncomfortable business?

He glanced at Fleming, who'd turned to study the chalkboard menu on the wall above the counter as if she held out hope there was something tastier up there than the mess on his plate.

Fleming knew how to hold on to hope.

## CHAPTER TEN

ABOUT A WEEK LATER, Jason left work early and found his way back to the home his parents had abandoned. Armed with an engineer's report and battery powered hanging lights, he inspected, starting with the roof of his house.

His house.

Maybe he was being foolish, even thinking of restoring this ruin. There were structural problems. Joists in the basement. Obviously, the porch stairs. But the second floor was apparently structurally sound. And the place belonged to him.

He could leave it rotting in the woods until it fell down, or he could rebuild it, but he already knew what he would do. He spent his working life restoring the derelict to functionality. That seemed to be his purpose.

After he restored a business, he moved on to the next one. Maybe it would be the same with this house, he thought wryly. A whole new business, flipping homes that had come to mean nothing to anyone.

He went to the porch steps. They rocked beneath his feet. He shouldn't have let Fleming in the place the other day. He reached down and pulled up one loose board. It came away, screaming when the rusty nails couldn't hold it in place.

He yanked another one off. Slowly, he stacked them all in a neat pile where no one could step on them and hit one of those nails. When there was nothing left except the supports the steps had rested on, he leaned down to inspect the crawl space.

Nothing in there that he could see, though the sun was getting low again. He straightened, listening to the wind sneak through all the openings vandals and squatters had left in the windows and walls.

What would his mother have done with this place if she'd kept it in the divorce? Would she have held on to it for all these years?

He stared at the house silently for a moment, then dragged his phone out of his pocket. He dialed his mother's number. She answered on the second ring.

"Jason, is this really you?"

"Hello," he said.

"Hi. I'm surprised."

"So am I." He'd considered rehabbing the house without contacting his long-lost mother, but it didn't seem right. "Why did you send me the toy?"

"Because you wanted it."

"Over twenty years ago."

"And I've had it that long."

"Why should I believe you?"

"I've never lied to you."

"Yeah. You took great care of me." He began pacing, fighting his own anger. "I didn't call about all that. I'm going to let you see the house if you want." He stopped. "You must have seen it if you still live in Bliss."

"I came back to Bliss about five years ago. I never expected to see you here. I was surprised to learn your grandparents moved to New York after I left."

"They wanted me to have family. Dad traveled a lot back then, and he worked long hours."

"I remember."

He nodded, though she couldn't see him. They were heading back into the past he still didn't want to discuss with her. "Have you seen the house?"

"The outside. It made me so sad I never went in."

"Well, you can if you want to."

"I don't know if I should. It might break my heart."

*What?* He didn't want to care about her broken heart.

Who had cared for her heart all these years? Someone had made her Mrs. Brown. "How's Bryce Danforth?"

"Gone. Years ago. He wanted something—someone—different. I only wanted to breathe again, so I didn't mind when he left."

"Great." Every mother's son wanted to hear she preferred fresh air to him. "I'll call you with a date and time to come out and look at the place. It's not safe right now to walk around in. I need to do a few repairs."

"Wait, Jason." Her urgency stopped him when he'd been on the verge of hanging up. "I can't afford to buy the house from you. I don't know what I was thinking when I said I wanted it back. Will you consider my offer to work there?"

"I'm really not comfortable with the idea

of you working for me so you have a place to live." He didn't mean to be rude, but they might as well get it straight that he wasn't falling for any Macland family machinations.

"It's too large for one single woman, anyway." She didn't seem to notice what he'd said.

He looked up. Two stories and a basement. An attic that had been converted into living space, and a large guesthouse apartment over the garage. It was a lot of room for any one person.

"When I make the floors safer, I'll call you back."

But now that he'd committed to it, he wasn't sure he wanted to follow through.

THE STORE WAS empty when Fleming's cell phone rang. It was late afternoon on a watery winter day, and the Christmas lights outside flashed colors on the faux snow in the windows and the dark-colored cushions of the window seats positioned in front of the displays. She grabbed her cell off the counter and answered.

"Are you coming?" Hugh asked without preamble. Her stepfather's anxious tone heightened Fleming's sense of guilt. "Your mother thinks you're working yourself to death on her account. She thinks that's why we haven't seen as much of you lately."

Had she stayed away from Knoxville more than usual? "I'm reluctant to leave for a weekend, but it's got nothing to do with Mom. I can't miss two whole days of sales at this time of year."

"Then just come to the party on Saturday evening. Skip the tree trimming on Friday afternoon. We'll be down there on Christmas Eve anyway."

"I hate to break our tradition, Hugh. I remember when you brought that first tree to our house. As old as I was, I still suspected you might be Santa."

He was silent for a moment. "Then come." He sounded a little fed up, but she knew he loved her as if he'd always been her father. "We both want you to."

Again, guilt swept Fleming. Hugh had given up an awful lot for her. He could have had a full-time wife years sooner if not for Fleming and her love for her home in the mountains. "I'll think about it. But I feel as if every minute I spend away from the store is a moment I'll regret."

"I understand that, but I'm going to tell you something I always tried to tell your mother, and I hope you'll listen a little better than she did. You have a life to live. Don't give it up for the store. Maybe that shop shouldn't be your first and only priority."

"Maybe." The thought made her sad. "But I'm not willing to give up on it."

"And I'm not asking you to. I'm asking you to give your mother the only gift she wants from you for Christmas. Your time."

"You're right. I know you are, but it doesn't make things easier."

"That Macland guy likes you. He's not going to close the store. He's gone out of his way to help you."

She turned away from the counter, trying to make sure no one else could hear his booming voice—as if he'd published his very wrong assumptions in the newspaper, and every friend or neighbor in Bliss could see them. As she did so, she saw the woman in the aqua uniform again, standing outside the window.

Too worried-looking to be creepy, she

roused Fleming's protective instincts. Maybe she could just give the woman whatever she wanted so badly she kept coming back.

Unwilling to turn her back in case her unknown visitor disappeared again, she started toward the front of the store. "Hugh, I feel as if Jason's already done too much for me, but even he can only go so far. He'll close the shop if the business isn't viable. He'll have no choice."

"Maybe that's for the best, Fleming. Why devote any more time or money to a lost cause?"

"I understand you mean well, but I'm going to save the store."

"I know you will."

She wasn't sure he meant it. "I'll call you and let you know if I'm coming."

She walked toward the door and smiled out at the woman, but the stranger seemed startled, and quickly turned away.

"Sorry," the woman said, throwing the word over her shoulder.

"No," Hugh said. "Just let me know you're on your way. Goodbye, Fleming. Call your mother more often."

"Okay." He was right about that last advice.

But when her news wasn't good, saying nothing was easier.

She hung up, slid the cell phone into the back pocket of her jeans and went outside. The cold air wrapped her in a frosty embrace, but the other woman had to be colder.

"Excuse me," she called. The retreating figure put on some speed, getting away from her. "Excuse me," Fleming said more loudly.

The woman whipped around the corner and disappeared like an hallucination.

What was so interesting about this store? And more to the point, who was she? Fleming didn't recognize her. She didn't think she'd ever seen her before that first night.

Shivering, Fleming went back inside. She studied the decorations, the lights twinkling around the glass insert in the door and around the plate glass windows. Quilts on rocking chairs, themed with Santas and snowmen. Red and green velvet bows on a red velvet sash looped along the building's Victorian molding. Christmas trees stationed around the floor.

Maybe the stranger was lonely during the holiday season, and was drawn to the warmth of Mainly Merry Christmas. With the crackling fire on the deep hearth as a cozy background, Fleming could see how someone might long to sink into the scene set by this store. She'd want one of everything.

But what Fleming needed was one or two customers with deep pockets.

The door jingled, and she turned, half expecting to see the woman entering. Instead, it was Jason, his gaze concerned.

"Hi," she said, in a breathy gasp.

He laughed. The sound was as rich as a cup of steaming hot chocolate. "What's wrong?"

"Nothing." She didn't intend to admit she had an issue with a window-shopper. "I'm glad to see you."

"Thanks." He didn't seem entirely convinced. "I hadn't planned to come in, but you looked as if you had a problem."

"So you thought you'd come solve it?" She regretted the question and her tone instantly. "I'm sorry. That was unkind. This place is my problem."

He nodded. "I wish I could do something more to help you."

She twisted her hands behind her back, linking them to keep from wringing them together where he could see. "Everything will be fine."

"What are you planning next?"

"I have ornaments coming. They were delivered to the wrong address in a town in west Tennessee, but they're on their way again. And wrapping," she said. "A wrapping station right out on the sales floor. We have a ton of paper left from last year. Vintage designs that apparently I loved more than any customers did." Sometimes she thought she'd been born in the wrong decade. "I'll wrap packages from the time the store opens until I lock the doors at night if that's what it takes to drag people in here."

"Will you charge them per package?"

"No, I've paid for the paper and taken the loss already, and if they continue to shop while they wait for me to wrap, I may make a few extra sales."

"I guess you can't afford to hire someone to wrap for you."

"No. It kind of stinks."

"Get your mom down here."

Hugh's call replayed in Fleming's mind. "She can't come back right now. She and Hugh have an annual holiday party. She starts planning it at the end of the summer, and she's at high speed right now."

"You aren't invited?"

His surprise made her laugh. He wasn't staying in Bliss, and he didn't intend to get involved with anyone, but he cared about her. She sobered when she realized he might think her family was like his—painfully detached. "I'm invited, but I don't want to take the time away from here."

He unbuttoned his coat. "You have to go to your parents' party."

Everyone had advice for her tonight.

He smiled at a woman walking past the store, who eyed them with curiosity. Fleming glanced between the two of them. She didn't know her. Another indebted bank customer, maybe?

"Fleming, how old are you?" Jason asked.

"I'm surprised the information isn't in my loan paperwork."

"Just tell me. How many years have you been on this earth?"

"Why do you want to know?"

He stared at her, and the silence suggested she just answer the question.

"Twenty-four," she said.

"Twenty-four Christmases with a mother who loves you so much she's put you ahead of her own needs and wishes for most of those years."

"Are you trying to make me feel guilty? Because Hugh already did that."

"I'm trying to remind you what you've told me about regret."

Twenty-four days out of all those thousands in a lifetime. It wasn't that much time for her mother to ask. "We're not talking about Christmas Day. They'll come down here then. This is just for a party for their friends and Hugh's colleagues."

"And they want you to come," Jason said.

"Has anyone asked you to go home for the holidays?" she asked, but Jason didn't answer, and he looked as if he wasn't going to. She didn't want to push. "Knoxville is a long way to drive, and I'll get back late," she said.

"I'll drive you." If he was angry she'd asked the hurtful question, he wasn't holding a grudge. "I'm not doing anything this weekend, and I could use a break from the accusatory looks I get in the diner when I go out for breakfast."

"You have a lousy job to do at this time of year."

"I'm starting to think for any time of year."

She felt bad for him. It couldn't be easy facing all the hurt people in Bliss. "You wouldn't mind coming with me?"

"You'd consider letting me?" He tugged at his tie.

Jason always looked as if he was working in a New York City bank, not the spot his great-grandfather had dug into the limestone of this little town.

"They really want me to go," she said, "and I don't mind the drive so much if I've got company. Plus, if you come with me, Hugh won't push all the eligible young interns he can find my way with jokes about mistletoe."

"Maybe he thinks you'd be better off with an eligible intern than stuck up here by yourself on this mountain."

"He's a dad. He worries. He called me a little while ago, and he kept trying to suggest I'm putting the store before my own life."

"He probably doesn't want you to be caught in the same trap as your mom."

"I don't look at it that way. It's my job."

"It keeps you buried in this town. What's here for you, Fleming?"

"Are you talking to me or to yourself?" How could they go from friendly to confrontational so swiftly? "Not everyone needs to be in a new place every month. I love this place and these people. I love my work, and I don't need anyone to take care of me."

"I don't doubt you. If the store can be saved, I believe you can do it. It's the 'why' I don't understand."

She gave in a little. "I know. This place seems stagnant to you. And to Hugh, as well." She had to smile, ruefully. "He's just trying to take care of Mom and me."

Jason wisely switched topics. "So when do we go to this shindig?" He glanced at his watch.

She must be keeping him from something. Like starving some widows and children. Fleming stopped herself. Why be unkind to him now, even in her thoughts?

The woman who'd taken to staring into her store had unsettled her. Hugh's advice made her question herself, and Jason's continued inability to see the good things about Bliss frustrated her, but he'd offered her a favor.

"The shindig is Saturday. We can leave here at four and make it to the party fashionably tardy."

"Sounds good. You know we have caroling practice on Saturday?"

"Family commitments qualify as an excused absence." Fleming watched him tighten his tie and tug the lapels of his black overcoat into place. She had an urge to go up on tiptoe and kiss his cheek. An innocent thank-you to make up for her angry thoughts.

Instead, she moved around the counter. "I'll pay for our gas and coffee on the road."

"You better believe it," he said.

## *CHAPTER ELEVEN*

ON SATURDAY, they arrived late, due to traffic, and Fleming seemed nervous as she danced across the parking lot to her parents' apartment building. Jason turned back, holding out his key fob to lock the car doors. He caught up with her as she reached the foyer.

"What's up with you?" he asked as they stepped into the elevator.

"I don't know. I get like this. They have their friends there, and they want me to be all interesting, but I'm just me. I feel like a sore thumb."

"You're interesting. Certainly not an introvert."

She punched the button to take them to the tenth floor. "I'm not sure how you'd know that." She studied herself in the reflective metal walls and primped her hair a little. She fascinated him, a mixture of indifference to her own beauty and the will to look good for Katherine and her husband's sake.

"You really don't want to be at this party, do you? I'm not sure you were this nervous in my office, talking mortgage terms."

"I always come to please my mother, and I'm glad that Hugh considers me his daughter and wants to show me off to his friends. My own dad was never that proud I was his." She tugged at the scarf around her throat. "What are you going to say when Hugh starts giving you the once-over because you came with me?"

"I'm here to back you up." That wasn't bad. Not a commitment. Not a promise that they'd mean something to each other in the future. Not even a date. Just one friend having another's best interests at heart.

"Are you?" She ducked her head to hide a grin that made him smile. "Thanks," she said. "So if I decide to bolt—"

"Not sure why you would, but I'd remind you that bolting would not please your mother or your stepfather."

"You understand more about Christmas than I thought you did—oh, no." She looked at Jason's empty hands. "Where's the wine?"

"I'm sorry—I forgot it in the car. You go ahead. I'll go back for it," he offered as the doors opened on the tenth floor.

Fleming hesitated, her hand stopping the elevator from closing. "All right. I'll see you inside. They're the only apartment on this level."

Fleming's stepfather must be even more successful than Jason had understood. He wondered why she hadn't asked him for help… maybe a loan of some kind. "See you in a few minutes."

The doors began to shut, sliding along their track.

Fleming smiled, but tonight she was the one who looked as if she was alone and lonely. "I thought you had my back," she accused.

IT WAS A silly thing to say, even as a joke. She wished she'd kept the thought inside her head where it had sounded funnier, but somehow going to her mother's door with a handsome, self-assured man at her side had seemed easier than just showing up alone like the spinster daughter she felt she was.

A sore thumb of the greatest magnitude.

She didn't need a man. It was ridiculous. What year was this?

But Jason wasn't just any man. He was the guy who showed up when she needed a boost, a taller person to reach the awning where her Christmas lights hung, the guy who went back for the wine. He was the man who'd tried to help her.

He was also the man who didn't mean to stay in Bliss, so she'd better not let herself feel any more than she already did.

Throwing back her shoulders as if preparing for a high jump, she walked to the door and pushed the doorbell.

A previous tenant had installed a chime that played "There's No Place Like Home." Fleming and Hugh thought it was funny, but her mother hated it, so they never used the bell unless a party was going on and knocking got drowned out by noise.

Everyone inside laughed at the song, too. Fleming was smiling as Hugh opened the door.

Behind him, people milled, men and women in their holiday finery. She caught the glitter of diamonds in earlobes and shiny, newly done hair. Formal gowns mixed with cocktail dresses and nice suits along with one or two tuxedos.

"You came." Hugh hugged her as if she were a gift. She recognized "The Holly and the Ivy" playing on the sound system. "Come in, come in." He dragged her over the doorstep and craned his head, searching for Katherine. "Your mother started to doubt, but I told her you wouldn't let her down. You should have brought a friend. Are you staying the night?"

"I brought someone, but we can't stay the night. I have to open the store tomorrow, and he always has a mountain of paperwork."

Hugh straightened. "Do I know this guy?"

"He's not a date, Hugh." She shrugged her coat off. "It's Jason, and we're really just acquaintances."

"The bank's hired gun?" Hugh sized up the situation with a wry smile. "The one who might evict you? I was joking when I said he liked you too much to close the doors on the shop."

"But you were sort of right. I'm sure Mom told you how he helped me with the loan."

"Why would you bring him? I want her

to enjoy Christmas, not have to face the guy who's causing her sleepless nights."

"Is she having trouble sleeping?" Fleming hoped not. "You should try to distract her from worrying about me. I'm working hard, and things are going all right. They could be better, but they're all right."

"Will that be enough? What does your banker friend say?"

"He seems as hopeful as we are, but that could be wishful thinking." Which didn't seem like Jason's style. "But be nice to him, Hugh. He doesn't have anyone in Bliss. Not even in Tennessee, really." She thought about his mother, but let the thought fade away. The woman must have come to Bliss after she heard about Jason's arrival, or surely Fleming would have heard of her by now. "Anyway, I thought he'd enjoy some Christmas spirit with us, and he offered to come."

"He won't try to talk business with your mother?"

"You mean will he offer me another deal I can't refuse through her?"

Hugh cracked a smile. "Is he that kind of banker?"

"He's not a banker. He understands bank-

ing, but he's a consultant who fixes sick businesses, and he seems like an honest guy. I
don't think he's enjoying his current job." She
held up her coat. "Not that he'd be spreading
his doubts around if he had any. Where can
I hang this? Is the closet full?"

"I'll put it away. Your friend's meeting you
here? He didn't come with you?" He took the
coat and wrapped it over his arm.

"We drove from Bliss together. I brought
some wine, but we forgot it in his car so he's
gone back for it."

"Honey." Her mother materialized from
the crowd of happy, laughing guests. "You
came. I'm so glad. How was the drive? You
look lovely."

"Thanks, Mom." She'd owned this dress
for at least four years. It was starting to look
like a schoolgirl's best. Acquaintance or not,
she wanted to look good for—with—Jason.
He'd go home and maybe he'd talk about the
backwoods woman from Tennessee who still
dressed as if she were on her way to a college formal.

Or maybe he'd forget her the second he
crossed the city limits, never to return.

"There's No Place Like Home" rang out, and her mom sighed.

"One day I'll persuade Hugh to change that thing."

"That'll be Jason, Mom."

"Jason?" Katherine's brows arched as she reached for the doorknob. "When did you start seeing him?"

"I'm not seeing him. Please don't embarrass me. He's not staying in Bliss, and I don't need a matchmaker, not you or Hugh."

"I'm not matchmaking. I notice you say he's not staying?"

"He's not."

"So you've asked?"

"I don't have to. He's been clear about it from the start."

"And that matters to you. Oh, dear. I have clearly been too uninvolved in your life."

*Thank goodness*, thought Fleming, because unfortunately, she feared she was getting serious about her feelings for Jason. "Mom, I'm begging you to be careful. Don't say anything mean to him. Don't be unkind about his job."

"You're the one who brought Scrooge to my party." Katherine had yanked the door open. Jason had to have heard. Unless he'd gone deaf. Hardly the kind of holiday joy to wish on anyone.

"Ho ho humbug," Jason said.

Fleming envied him his cool.

"I DIDN'T MEAN IT. What I said earlier." Katherine passed Jason a glass of wine when they finally met up again. Fleming had towed him around the room, introducing him to her parents' friends. "I just meant that your job requires you to be a sort of Scrooge to the people in Bliss who—" She stopped.

"May lose their homes or businesses." He finished the thought for her. He took the glass and sipped. "I've thought of that a time or two."

"I'm sorry. I was incredibly rude. I can only blame my lack of manners on my concern for Fleming."

"You mean because she brought me this evening?"

Katherine measured him with a look, as if she wasn't quite sure what to expect from him, and he turned to search for Fleming. What was going on with her that had made her mother so overprotective?

"I worry that she's giving up her dreams

to support mine." Katherine clearly wasn't sharing the whole truth. He read people well enough to know when someone was hiding something. "I probably shouldn't have told you that."

If Fleming had other dreams, she was keeping them close to the vest. What were they, if not the store? "I know how hard she's working. She must want that shop. Maybe more than even you know."

"Probably." She turned, a little harried. But she was a hostess, and this was a large gathering. She had a lot on her mind. "What can I get you? Are you hungry?"

"I'm fine, Katherine."

"Where has Fleming gone?"

"She's talking to her stepfather." Jason nodded toward Fleming and the stocky man. Fleming glanced his way. He nodded. She smiled, a blush coloring her cheeks.

They were a couple tonight. He'd brought her. She'd come with him. They were together. Just for tonight—no past, no future.

He took another wineglass from a passing server. "Will you excuse me, Katherine?" he said.

"She doesn't like wine." Katherine plucked

the second glass from his fingers. "She usually arrives early at a party, and she asks for cranberry juice in a nice glass. It's not exactly the right color, but most people don't notice."

"Why?" he asked.

"Why what?" Katherine smiled. "Why the wine? Why the juice?"

"Why try to pass one off for the other? I wouldn't have thought Fleming cared what other people thought about her."

"She was in college when she turned twenty-one. All her friends embraced drinking, but it just never appealed to her, and she said she felt like the odd woman out. She told me she had a friend who called her their token temperance crusader. She doesn't care about drinking—I mean, she doesn't think there's anything wrong with it. She just doesn't enjoy the taste."

"I still can't imagine her pretending to be someone she isn't."

Katherine tsked at him. "She would never do that. She's the most honest woman I know. Just a little quirky."

He held up both hands. "We seem determined to misunderstand each other. I'm sorry."

"So am I. Let me get Fleming for you."

"Katherine, I don't need you to get her." He touched her arm, gently, because she seemed so wary, even here in her own home. "I'm sorry we've gotten off to such an uncomfortable start tonight."

"That's my fault. I love my daughter. I'd do anything for her, and I'm concerned about her future."

He took a sip of his wine. That was a concept foreign to him, a parent worrying and fighting for their child's happiness. "I don't know you very well, but I respect the fact that you love your daughter, and that you appreciate the store for what it gave you when you needed a living."

She nodded. "That's right."

"You don't have to be afraid I'm going to shut down the place on a whim, or push Fleming to keep it until she can't get out of it without losing everything."

"Because you might lose your job if the bank fails?"

"I couldn't care less about that," he said, and in that moment, he meant it. His family's bank mattered to his father. It was a consultancy for him.

"You don't care right now because you want to get along with Fleming's family and friends, and I assume you're decent enough to hate what this job is doing to people already in financial trouble. But later, if your reputation is involved…"

"My reputation is always involved. I get new work via word of mouth from satisfied clients, but I've never pushed anyone to undertake business they couldn't handle."

A palm touched the small of his back, and suddenly, he was deeply in the present, aware of Fleming's touch, yes, but also of the scent of gingerbread, the glitter of the tinsel, and the wrapping paper on the gifts beneath Katherine and Hugh's tree.

This was what a Christmas could be. Family, looking out for each other, caring. This was what it should be. But it was also what he'd missed since the earliest holidays he could remember.

"Mom, what are you saying to Jason? I thought we were celebrating the season tonight, but you seem to be talking business." Fleming glanced at the glasses on a tray that sailed by on a server's hand. "Maybe you should have a bite to eat and a drink. And try to let down your guard."

"I know," Katherine said. "I get nervous and I talk too much. I'm not myself tonight."

"What's up?" Fleming asked.

"Nothing." Katherine made a valiant effort to shake off her concerns. "I've behaved in a shocking manner toward Jason, and I should be apologizing, rather than making my excuses."

Seeing Fleming's deepening concern, he backed up and touched her arm. "I'll give you two a few minutes."

He took a turn around the room, moving anywhere the two women were not. A set of glass doors were thrown open onto the balcony, presumably to allow cool December air inside the stuffy apartment. A man and woman drifted outside.

Jason crossed to the bar and asked for a beer and some juice in a wineglass. Afterward, he saw Katherine and Fleming standing together, apart from the crowd.

"Just in time," Katherine said as he returned. "I think we were on the verge of an ugly argument." She smiled, bringing to mind the old saying about there being truth in every slightly bitter joke. "I must see to my guests. You two have a lovely evening. If you decide you want to stay, we have plenty of room, and we'd love to have you both."

She sailed away, pulling poise around herself like a jacket.

"I like your mother. She just wants you to make choices that give you the best life. I don't mean to sound as if I'm offering sage advice from behind my desk, but you want her to live her life, and she's trying to help you live a safe one. I understand you're both trying to make things right for each other." Jason passed the glass of juice to Fleming. "Your own special concoction," he said.

Confusion passed over her face. "Mom told you about the juice. You probably think I'm immature and ridiculous."

"I think you prefer juice."

She paused, but then laughed, and her laughter bathed him in familiarity. They might not get along smoothly 100 percent of the time, and they might want different things from life, but they met somewhere in the middle. In some ways they were like calling to from the isolation of two lonely lives.

Maybe Jason was right in his outlook, refusing to see possibilities. Loneliness was not a rock-strong foundation.

"My mother feels guilty because as soon as she sold me the store, we started having problems," Fleming said, taking the glass from his hand. Her fingers brushed his, though she didn't seem to notice. "She was just quizzing me on sales figures. This should be our best month. That's why she's worried. If we can't turn a profit in December, she fears we're doomed."

"She might have a point," he said. "But remind your mom that the first payment on the new loan isn't due until February. You have time if you really want it, Fleming."

He couldn't help encouraging her, because he didn't want her to worry. He wanted to save the holiday for her.

"Why do you and my mother keep treating me as if I'm playing store in my spare time? I'm working as hard as I can to make a living. I'm invested, and I'm not sure why I have to prove it to either of you. You're not involved. Remember?" She sipped her cranberry juice and her lips pursed, making him smile instead of reacting to her taunt.

It wasn't the time or the place, and she had a point.

"You don't like that stuff, either?" he asked.

"I like the way it hits the front of your mouth. Orange juice gets you in the back of your throat, but cranberry is more intense."

"You talk as if it's a fine wine."

"And you managed to change the subject." She held out her hand. "Come with me. I'll show you my very first Christmas ornament. You'll understand Mom better when you see she's kept every ornament she's given me since the year I was born."

"I thought mothers did that to give them to their children as a start on their own collection of ornaments."

"Mom's different. Maybe she'll pass them along one day, but right now, she likes to relive my childhood via the ornaments. We end up talking about them every Christmas season. Same stories every year."

"You don't want to hear them?" he asked, and suddenly, old memories flashed through his mind, images of a big, red, metal fire truck, or the window he'd sat in, blowing to fog the glass so he could write his name with his finger. He'd waited for his own mother in that window until he was so cold he was shivering, and his grandmother had appeared, insisting he needed to warm up in bed before Santa came.

"I love hearing them over and over. We travel through the good years and the bad ones until we reach the present, which always seems more hopeful on Christmas Eve. Mom suggests it'll be the same for me when I have children of my own. Then I'll want them to know who I was, and I'll need to remember—and according to her, I'll bore the daylights out of them with the stories she's told me."

Fleming didn't sound as if she minded the idea. They'd slowly circled the room together as they talked, and they ended up in front of the tree.

"I wonder if she's right." Jason palmed a small, perfectly recreated train that fitted as if it were made for his hand. "I do wonder who my parents were."

"Why your mother left, and why your father didn't go after her and drag her back to your home, where she belonged?"

He turned to look into Fleming's face. Knowledge gleamed in her gaze. "That's what you thought about your own parents?"

he asked. "Even though you knew what your father was like?"

"I don't think anyone should be dragging anyone else, but yeah, I wonder why my father chose to disappear from my life for so long." She glanced her mother's way as if thinking about her birth father was somehow a betrayal. "How could I help wondering why he didn't love Mom and me? A lot of the kids I knew had divorced parents, but they all had two of them. Fathers showed up every other weekend, maybe baffled about what they were supposed to do, sometimes forgetting treats for soccer practice, but they were there—and happy to be with their children."

Jason didn't want to look her in the eye. He was afraid of what his own expression might expose. "You remember those times more at the holidays. When you see other families together, enjoying each other, it's hard not to wonder what went wrong with your own."

Fleming moved around the tree.

"This is my first ornament." She touched a small woven basket that held a pink-diapered baby whose dark red curls were disheveled by time or small hands that had touched them too often. "Mom told me she and my father chose it together. I was born in October, and I like to think they were still happy, at least when they found this."

"It's well loved," he said, wishing for her sake that Hugh's obvious affection for her could have been enough to heal all the wounds her birth father had inflicted.

"I guess I kept looking into that basket," she said, putting it back. Then she bent and took another ornament off a low-hanging branch.

This one was a small, white clapboard house on a platform of snow. Smoke curled out of the chimney. A Christmas tree blinked chips of brightly colored glass as lights just off the porch. The windows glowed with golden light that flickered as if it came from candles. "This one's my favorite. That glow was like love to me coming from the imaginary family that lived there. I made up stories about lots of families who might have lived in this house."

"How old were you when your mother gave you that one?"

"I bought it myself when I was seventeen."

"You made up your own family at seventeen," he said, with no attempt at subtlety.

Her smile wasn't real. Her gaze shifted away from his. "Maybe we've talked enough."

"Maybe the reason we talk so much is that you know I'm leaving, and I don't doubt you're staying."

"You're saying in yet another way that we're off-limits to each other." Fleming turned back to the tree. Her shoulders seemed to droop a little as she put the ornament back. Her hands seemed fragile, the small bones vulnerable, as she slipped the ornament's sturdy gold cord around a branch. "But what I don't know is why you continue to run. You don't have to leave Bliss. You can live anywhere you want, and I know you're getting attached."

"Attached?" He felt as if he was holding his breath. No one made him feel like this. He didn't want to. It was like suffocating.

"To the town. To your house." She flicked a glance over her shoulder. "To some of the people who live in Bliss."

Which ones? Deep inside, he faced the truth. Only one person. Fleming mattered to him. Fleming's feelings were important, and he'd protect her from any more hurt if he could.

"I'm curious about the town, and the past I don't remember. My family had a place there once. I don't."

"You've started building a life there, even if you never meant to." She froze, as he tried to understand whether she was asking for a commitment he didn't know how to make. "Or maybe I've said too much again."

He turned her around, making sure he was gentle. He touched her hair, drawn to the silky texture because he'd never touched a woman so soft and so vibrant with life. Everything about her was different. "I like your town, and I've tried to help the people. I care about you, but Bliss is not my home. I don't want to be tied down."

Fleming looked up at the tree, not at him. "Why is living somewhere being tied down? Bliss could be your home if you chose. You only have to want to stay somewhere."

"But I don't." He wouldn't lie to her, and even her suggestion that he could choose to stay in one job in one place made his feet itch to travel. "Staying is not my strong point."

"But why? Why do you choose to leave

the place that belongs to you? Whether it's New York where your family lives or here, why do you choose to leave the people who care about you?"

"Because I'm not the kind of man who inspires that kind of love," he said. "And maybe I don't know how to give it. I get bored. With the same work, the same faces, the same people."

It might be brutal, but it would be crueler to pretend. She deserved more and better than a guy who lied to make her care for him.

Fleming reached out and touched the small house with her index finger. She didn't speak. He didn't push her.

She knew what he had to offer. Right now, and nothing more.

Suddenly, with energy that startled him, she turned. Her smile was as false as any lie he could have told her. "I'm staying here tonight. Mom will drive me home in the morning in time to open the store."

She touched his sleeve, above his hand. The way she'd say goodbye to a customer she knew well, but not intimately. Her warmth was not real.

"Thank you for coming with me tonight. I

enjoyed our talk. Be safe getting back through the mountains."

With that, she turned and was gone.

Jason felt empty. He wanted to be with this beautiful, selfless woman, but he was no match for her. He wanted his own life, privacy, to come and go as he pleased, with no commitments. And no expectations.

She didn't seem to understand he was offering her ultimate freedom, as well. They could choose to be together, but they didn't have to spout the ridiculous promises people made to each other. And then always broke.

"Excuse me. I believe you're Jason Macland?"

The stocky man who'd given Fleming's mother the freedom to choose her own unconventional way of life stood at Jason's shoulder.

"I am," he said.

"My daughter asked me to tell you goodnight."

"I'm leaving. You don't have to throw me out."

Hugh's smile tilted. "That was the impression she gave me, too—that I should make sure the door closed behind you. I don't understand, and I don't mean to be rude. You can't see her again, because she told me she's going to bed, but you're welcome to food and drink." Hugh turned, opening his hand to the room, like the ringmaster in a circus. "And to fellowship with our friends."

"Thanks." Jason offered his hand. "I should be going. I have a long drive."

"Well, good night, then. Let me walk you to the door. I don't see my wife anywhere."

If he knew Katherine at all, she'd hurried down the hall toward the bedrooms, close on Fleming's heels. "Thank her for her hospitality. And thank you. I enjoyed this evening."

"Somehow I don't think so," Hugh said. "But I'm glad we had a moment to speak. I wanted to thank you for all you've done for Fleming. I wish she would have accepted my help, but I am grateful that you've offered her your assistance."

"I may not have done her a favor." Jason had to admit, finally, that he'd put extra effort into finding a loan that would work for Fleming because he'd been drawn to her from that first moment in his office. She'd become a part of his life, an urgent requirement he was determined to ignore.

He wasn't ready to make the commitment

she needed. He was still the guy who had her business in his hands. "I'll have to foreclose if she misses payments."

Hugh all but sputtered. "Well," he managed to say, his face ruddy for a renowned cardiologist, "Merry Christmas to you."

# CHAPTER TWELVE

THAT WOMAN HAD come by the store again. It was Monday night. Fleming made a note. Maybe the woman had a pattern. Something had to be wrong to draw her back again and again, and then send her away without her saying a word.

Whatever was going on, the third visit finally spooked Fleming. She circled the store, locking doors and windows and turning down the lights so she could see out better than anyone could see inside.

She set the alarm and hurried out the back, unable to escape the feeling that she was being watched. She was letting that woman get in her head.

The fact that she was fleeing from an as-yet-imaginary threat didn't ease her anxiety. She parked on the mountain, right in front of her house. No one had followed her. She was positive of that, but her hands shook as she shivered in the cold night air, trying to find her keys in the depths of her purse.

She'd forgotten to turn on the porch lights, and she jabbed at the keyhole a few times before she found the sweet spot and unlocked the door. The same key unlocked the dead bolt. She rushed inside, spooked by her own panic as much as by the wind howling around her, lifting her hair with rough hands. After she locked the door and twisted the dead bolt, she leaned against the door, laughing at her own foolishness.

Nevertheless, she checked the lock again. Even without strangers peeking into her store on a semi-nightly basis, she was sometimes a little antsy living up here on the mountain alone. The house that had been so warm and cozy and loving with her mother just down the hall, or puttering in the kitchen, could feel empty when Fleming was on her own.

She dropped her purse and keys and took off her coat to drape it over the straight-backed chair beside the desk in the hallway. Then she made her way to the kitchen. A quick survey of the refrigerator reminded her she should have stopped to pick up something she could make for dinner.

"Thank goodness for cheese and eggs," she said, to break the echoing silence. She ought to get a puppy. Or a cat. A nice, big cat which would occupy itself when Fleming worked long hours, but be glad to have treats and company when she made it home.

Because she wanted to be a cat lady in a Christmas town.

As she was reaching for the eggs, the front doorbell rang. She jumped, but decided it was probably just the paper delivery guy, who always came in person instead of dropping off a pay envelope at the holidays. But when she opened the door, Jason stood outside, snow in his dark hair, his hand and most of his arm hidden by the thick branches of a beautifully scented fir tree.

"Merry Christmas." He tilted the tree toward her.

"For me?"

She hadn't put up a tree at home in years, not since her mother had started spending the holidays at Hugh's place. Fleming went to Knoxville to be with her mom and Hugh when they decorated, and when they came home, they had a little miniature one she usually set on a chest in the hall. They'd all agreed it was being together that counted, but she felt a surge of happiness at the thought of decorating her own tree.

"I owe you. For going to the house with me."

A little burr of disappointment troubled her. She'd rather he just wanted to give her a tree and help her decorate it. But that was a thing couples did when they were beginning to build a future together.

"Come in," she said, and reached to help him carry his gift.

"I can get it if you'll just hold the door."

He eased the tree past her, but stopped the moment he was over the threshold. "I don't think it's tall enough."

"It's perfect." She breathed deeply, relishing the wintery perfume. "Let's take that binding off." She pulled at the blue netting that held the tree's limbs. "I'll get some scissors."

"Your ceilings are twelve feet or more."

"This tree is perfect." She glanced into his face, but his eyes, warm and hopeful, made her feel self-conscious. She hurried to the kitchen to search for shears. "No one's ever done something like this for me."

"No guy, you mean," he said, as if that didn't mean anything, comparing himself to some random guy from her past. "Your parents must have brought home Christmas trees."

Thank goodness he hadn't made it to the kitchen before she got herself under control. *No one's ever done this*... What had happened to her brain?

She heard his footsteps. He was heading her way. She needed to find her composure.

"Yes, I meant no guy." She pivoted and he was behind her. She looked him square in the face. If he turned away, so be it. This gift touched her. She wanted to thank him for his kindness. "And I'm glad you're here. I was feeling a little off tonight."

"Maybe I was lonely too." He did glance away then, as if loneliness, their single common trait, was too dangerous to admit.

But she wasn't foolish. Loneliness was still no foundation.

"Where should we set it up?" she asked, hoping he planned to stay.

The kitchen was separated from the dining room and living room by a wide hall. Fleming thought for a minute. She often worked on her laptop in the living room, but sometimes worked at the dining room table.

Easy decision. Christmastime. A fireplace and this beautiful tree. "The living room." She led the way. "I have to find the stand."

He came into the room after her. "It's a little chilly in here."

"Old house. Old heating and air system. I'll turn up the thermostat."

"Or I could start a fire," he said, tilting the tree as if pointing with it.

The hearth looked big and empty and cold. She'd been living here, but not really living. Existing, cooking, cleaning. But not truly enjoying the lovely things about the home that had been hers since childhood.

"A fire would be nice." She reached out to take the tree from him, but he helped her lean it in the corner by the hearth. "I have some seasoned wood out back," Fleming said. "It's in the shed by the fence."

"Is this shed locked?"

She laughed at the idea. "Mom always said someone would have to be intent on stealing firewood to come all the way up here, climb the fence to our backyard and then search the shed." She did have a second's uneasiness, but the mystery woman would not have walked all the way up the mountain.

"You don't keep anything else in the shed?"

"A lawnmower, powered by human feet and hands." She laughed. "The kind with revolving blades, but no motor, that you have to push. Really vintage."

"You should maybe sell that," he said, with a grin that pleased her, making her feel unexpectedly close to him. "You might get a good price from an antiques dealer."

"You're making fun of me again?"

"A little."

"Besides, I can't get rid of it. I'd have to buy a goat to eat the grass come spring."

His smile widened, and her heart softened. "I'll get the wood," he said with a sweet tone of indulgence.

"I'll find the tree stand."

Was the box of Christmas ornaments upstairs in the attic or down in the basement? Ridiculous that she didn't even know. Those ornaments hadn't been unpacked since her mother had chosen her favorites to take to Knoxville, maybe six years ago.

Fleming ran up the stairs toward the attic first. Less creepy than the spidery basement.

In the hall between the linen press and the guest room, she yanked on the pull cord that brought down the attic stairs.

The floor up there was made of wide, unwaxed planks, and a slightly musty, dusty smell pervaded. She was practically on her hands and knees as she reached the top of the stairs and clambered into the attic.

As a child, she'd loved this place. Her mother had stored her own childhood books up here, along with toys that Fleming had handled with a careful touch. For some reason, her mother had never brought those toys out of the attic. They'd been a rainy or snowy day treat when the warm attic was a more hospitable place.

Fleming tried to ignore the books that always beckoned her from their shelves along the walls, and started with the closest boxes. She found old clothing and discarded window treatments, and cookbooks dotted with tomato sauce, dried batter and oily spots.

She opened the top of another box to discover her old school notebooks. She shut that one quickly. No reliving the past, awakening those aged memories. Jason had come to decorate a Christmas tree, not to stroll down her memory lanes.

He might have come only to help set up the tree.

She straightened, spying a box beneath the circular window, one with a Christmas tree sketched in green crayon on it.

She'd drawn that when she was too young to remember doing it. "Got it," she yelled, uncertain whether Jason was even back in the house.

There were three boxes of decorations in all, but Fleming found the stand in the first one she opened, and dragged it to the edge of the pull-down ladder stairs. She grabbed the next one, not even sure what was in it. She'd managed to ease the first box halfway down the steps when Jason arrived.

"Wait a minute," he said. "You don't look steady up there. How heavy is that?"

"I'm fine."

"No. You're not. Let me carry it."

He climbed the lower rungs and took the box from her hands. She reached back for the second box, but Jason was on the ladder behind her when she started to turn.

His breath warmed her face as he looked at

her. It felt like he was crowding her, but at the same time managing to hold his body away from hers in the extremely small space. His eyes were level with hers for the first time, and she noticed one dark fleck in the jade-green iris of his right eye.

"Hi," she said, as unnerved as if she'd bumped into her secret crush in high school.

"Why won't you ever let anyone help you?"

"What do you mean?"

He reached for the box that she was all but holding over their heads. "Not your mom with the store, not me until you have no choice. Not Hugh. You won't even let me help you carry these boxes. They're too heavy."

"I've got them," she said, with a small smile, trying to think of anything except how close he was, and how badly she wanted to lean into him.

Except that couldn't be what she wanted.

"Give me the box," Jason said.

She felt him lift it from her hands, and she let it go. "Thanks," she said.

"Uh-huh." He turned smoothly and adroitly and carried the box down to the landing.

Breathing as hard as if she'd run a race, Fleming didn't budge. She eased one breath and then another through her lips. *Get a grip. Find some control.*

They didn't need anything else from the attic tonight. She turned and backed down to the second floor. As soon as she reached it she bumped into Jason.

"Let me put the stairs back up," he said.

She hopped out of the way. Clearly, she was the only one feeling hyperaware, and it didn't mean anything. Except that she was lonely and the holidays had arrived, and maybe she envied the couples who strolled past the store each night, holding hands or carrying their children. Making families. Making dreams.

"Let's get started," Jason said. "Are you a control freak about decorating, or can we just go casual?"

"Huh?" Distracted, she tried to focus without staring too hard at the handsome, sculpted face that was beginning to mean too much to her.

"Do you start with lights, then go through your ornaments in a specific order and finally add the icicles, piece by piece? Or can we just put everything on as we take the decorations out of the box?"

"We don't have icicles. I used to have a

cat that ate anything that looked like string. We had to get rid of all that. We had a faux tree at the time, and we had to vacuum the icicles off it."

"I was using them as an example," he said. "No one reuses icicles."

"You're an expert in tree decoration?" She found her own personality again, stopped being dumbfounded and reached for one of the boxes.

"I watched the people my father hired to decorate our trees. They all had their methods. Every year until I left home for college, I wished someone would just once throw the ornaments on however they came out of the box."

"What would your dad have done?"

Jason arched an eyebrow as if he'd never thought about the question, but then shrugged. "He probably would have presented me with a schedule for deducting the decorators' overtime from my allowance, and then had them start over."

"Allowance... I'm not sure I knew a real person who got an allowance."

"How did your mom handle money?"

"I helped in the store. She 'paid' me." Fleming started down the hall, hitching the box to a more secure position in front of her. "But about the tree—we didn't have a decorating plan. We always just grabbed the Christmas ornaments and put them on the branches."

"That's the way to do it."

"And now's your chance." Fleming glanced over her shoulder. The box with the tree stand in it was heavier, but he picked it up as if it weighed nothing. "Tree decorators," she said. "I never heard of such a thing, but if I lose the store, maybe that's a whole new career direction."

JASON SET HIS BOX on the floor beside the tree, and Fleming swooped in, flushed and happy and infectiously ready to work.

She seemed to be unconscious of her charm or the sweetness of her sadness when she tried so hard in the store, but somehow always seemed to be behind on sales figures.

He often walked past her windows and saw her working on her laptop or setting up some new display. But when his assistant had said something to him about the irony of a woman who owned a Christmas store, yet gossip said she never decorated her own home, he'd been driven to do a ridiculous good deed.

The woman who owned the Christmas tree lot had given him time to search for the perfect tree. He'd wanted the right one for Fleming.

She shouldn't be without a tree at Christmas.

In the old days, banks used to give out toasters. They still did deals for their clients. Why shouldn't he buy a client a tree?

Fleming was a client. That was all. That was fine.

If he wanted to keep her in the client compartment of his life, he should not be hanging around her on her attic stairs or any other part of her house, wishing he had the right to kiss her.

"Would you like hot chocolate?" she asked from behind him, her voice as silky as the most expensive chocolate. "It's tradition. We brew it up and pop cookies in the oven."

"Always with the cocoa," he said. "But I really like cookies. What kind do you have?"

"Snickerdoodles or gingerbread. My mom always had her own dough in the freezer this time of year." Fleming turned toward the kitchen. "I have store-bought. Whenever I try to make homemade, I always seem to leave something out of the mix. Cream of tartar, essence of this or that."

He followed her because she was still talking, and he didn't know what else to do. This evening was beginning to feel ever so slightly like a date.

"Once, I was chewing on these slightly dry oatmeal-raisin cookies I'd just pulled out of the oven, and when I opened the microwave to warm my coffee, I discovered the congealed butter I'd melted that I was supposed to put in the batter."

"So baking definitely isn't your dream?"

She laughed. "Having a baker friend who was dying to make me tasty treats whenever I wanted. That would be a dream."

He considered.

"Do you have chocolate chips and brown sugar?"

"Why?"

"Do you like real chocolate-chip cookies?"

She put one candy-apple-colored nail to the side of her cheek, pondering. "I love chocolate chip."

"I have a recipe." He started rolling up his

sleeves. He hadn't changed clothes after work. He'd been so eager to present his gift that he'd come over in the suit he'd worn to the office that day, and only shucked off his jacket after he'd dragged the tree from his car roof.

"In your head?" Fleming asked. "You've memorized it?"

"I have a brother and two sisters who are younger than I, and they liked cookies. I like cookies."

"I like a man who bakes cookies." She started opening cabinets and a wide pantry. "What else do you need?"

"Let me help you put the tree in the stand, and then I'll see if you have all the ingredients."

He liked that no one had ever brought her a tree before, and obviously no man had ever offered to bake for her.

She eased past him and back through to the living room, and her perfume went to his head. He watched her open the box to take out the stand, then he went to the tree and picked up the scissors she'd gotten earlier, to finish cutting the blue net that bound the branches.

"I think we should put it up now," he said,

"and while the cookies are baking, maybe the limbs will spring back."

"Sounds like a plan to me. I don't know why I've been so stubborn about Christmas trees before this. They seemed like too much trouble, but at this point, I'd tie bulbs onto a Charlie Brown tree and consider myself lucky."

"I'll hold the fir up. You tighten the pegs around the trunk."

"Okay."

With a bit of maneuvering, they managed. Fleming stood back and shook her head. "It's crooked. You're really patient. Hugh gives Mom and me three chances, and then it's done, straight or not. We've had to tie the tree to their staircase before."

"We did that once. My baby sister had a kitten, and it kept climbing and knocking the thing down. Dad said the tree was too ugly to keep, and threatened to throw it out, but my grandfather wouldn't allow it. Grandpa asked Dad what he had against the holidays, and why he was so determined to get rid of our tree, and then he managed to help us secure it."

"Your dad sounds…" Fleming bit that

candy-colored nail. "I'm sorry. Maybe I shouldn't offer my opinion so generously."

"He was detached." Jason heard the words come out of his mouth, and they shocked him. "He didn't mean any harm. The tree was in our nursery dining room. We didn't have the nicer ornaments, and he didn't really care what it looked like."

"Nicer ornaments?" Fleming stood back again, studying the tree. "What does that mean?"

"Is it straight?"

She formed the sign for "okay" with her fingers and thumb and they both laughed. Because they were together?

"What about those ornaments? You had nursery ones and big-people ones?"

"The ones on the big-people tree weren't to be broken," he said. "The others came down with cats and children, and sometimes the nanny, running after one or more of us."

"I don't believe your life," Fleming said. "Nurseries and nannies."

"You had your mom and Hugh."

"And I've become like your dad, detached about decorating at home. I only put my heart into the decorations at the store, and no one really enjoys those. They're just for selling."

"Well, you're changing that tonight," Jason said, rising and wiping small needles off his pant leg. "I can start the cookies while you take out the decorations."

"Why did you do this for me?" She was leaning over the ornaments box, but stopped, her hands falling to her sides as she straightened. "How did you know I wouldn't have a tree at home?"

He tried to come up with a plausible answer and even considered idiotically claiming he'd had a feeling. "Hilda," he finally said. "She loves your store, but apparently knows you well enough to be able to tell me you haven't been doing anything at home for the holidays."

Fleming's mouth thinned, but only for a second. Her smile was full and real and forgiving. "I don't mind that someone told you. You brought me this beautiful gift."

"I thought you should remember you were worth the trouble," he said.

She looked taken aback, and he wished he'd kept quiet this time.

"But you won't have a tree in your hotel room?" she asked.

"No, but who does?"

"Lots of folks. I see them in the windows every year as I walk to work from the parking lot. And when I go back to my car, the colored lights comfort me. If you don't have your own tree, you'll have to come here and enjoy this one. It's yours, really."

"Come here?" Join her in celebrating a family holiday? He'd been trying to just do a good deed, and she was assuming it meant more than that.

"Not if it scares you," she said, with a laugh that got under his skin. "I didn't take the tree as some sort of engagement talisman."

"I don't even know what that means," he said.

"Nothing." She went back to the boxes and opened the cardboard flaps on the one with the ornaments. Lifting them out, she acted as if the air wasn't suddenly full of tension. "I think I'll put these on the couch, and we can just hang them up willy-nilly."

"Sounds good."

He went to the kitchen and pulled down all the ingredients he needed. Her cabinets were neat. He hardly spent a month at a time in his apartment, and the kitchen looked fine on the surface, but open any door and the place was a shambles.

He was buttering the cookie sheets when she came in.

"Find everything you wanted?" she asked.

He nodded. "Want to help me scoop the dough?"

"Sure. Mom always uses an ice cream scoop. We have a couple."

"They'll make big cookies," he said.

"Big are best. They're always chewier."

"I never thought of that."

"And you're the expert." She opened a drawer and pulled out one silver handled scoop, and one with a yellow enamel handle. She offered him his choice, and he took the silver one.

"Why do you have two?"

"I don't know." Blowing her hair over her shoulder, she scooped cookie dough onto one of the sheets. "Maybe one was a gift, but I don't actually remember."

"Then why suggest it was a gift? You like to find a story for everything, don't you?"

She always blushed easily, but her face

flushed more intensely, as if he'd hit a nerve. About telling stories? He didn't get it.

"I'm curious." She cleared her throat. "I like to understand why people think the way they do. Why things are the way they are, so I come up with stories to explain them for myself."

"Do you? I like that."

She avoided his gaze. "When will these cookies be done?"

An hour later, they finished the tree, and Fleming turned off the living room lights. In the glow from the kitchen and hall, they sat together in front of the tree, and toasted their efforts with mugs of hot cocoa.

"Thank you," she said, offering him the plate of cookies. "You were so kind to do this. I was a little creeped out tonight, and I didn't want to be alone."

Jason's antenna went up. "Creeped out? What are you talking about?"

"You know, sometimes you get a little uneasy for no real reason. I was when I got home, but tonight was fun."

"Are you sure it was for no reason? Did something happen that bothered you?"

"No. My imagination got the better of me

and I—" She broke off. "Never mind. I feel silly even mentioning it."

"I don't know what we're talking about." He took the plate and cup from her and set them on the floor between them. "What happened?"

She thought for a second. Hard. He could see she didn't want to talk about whatever was bothering her.

"Fleming," he said.

She looked at him, looping her hair behind her ear. "There's this woman. I don't know who she is. She keeps coming by my store. Three times now. She stands at the window and stares in as if something's on her mind."

"Could she be one of my clients?" he asked. "Maybe she's thinking I gave her a raw deal and you got a better one. You mentioned yourself that people have said as much."

"Because we're friends. It used to bother me, but now, I don't care what anyone says. It's ridiculous." Fleming took a cookie and bit the edge. "But I still wonder about this woman. I don't know if she's in trouble or—I just don't know."

"What does she look like?"

"Tall, dark hair, very thin."

"How old?"

"I'm not good with age. Maybe sixty-ish?"

He thought, scanning his memory for a client who matched that description. "No. I don't remember anyone." He picked up his mug and took a thoughtful sip. And then suddenly, it hit him. Out of the blue. Out of the past. "My mother."

"What?" Fleming set the cookie back on her delicate china serving plate.

"My mother. If she knows where I've been, she knows you and I see each other a bit."

"You think she followed you to my shop?"

He had a gut feeling. "It's a pretty big coincidence that you're seeing this woman and I have a mystery mother somewhere in town."

"Why would she be hanging around my shop?" Fleming crossed her legs and wrapped her arms around herself. "She must be desperate to see you."

"I called her and told her she could come by the house. When she does, I'll talk to her."

"Jason, I don't need you to take care of me, and I can't be responsible for you being cruel to your mother."

"Cruel? Why would you think I'd be cruel to her?"

"Because she left you, and you don't seem inclined to forgive."

"I don't understand her, but I wonder if she's healthy—if she is the one who's been hanging around your store, making you feel uncomfortable, that is."

"Don't hurt her feelings."

"You seem convinced I really am some sort of Scrooge."

"I don't want to be the source of someone else's pain."

She robbed him of the power of speech. In his world people fought the ones who hurt or frightened them. People sought payback. It was the reason he stayed out of messy relationships. He'd had plenty of payback because his own family couldn't seem to mix.

He'd never seen the need to complicate his life further. But Fleming was a complication that tempted him more and more.

# CHAPTER THIRTEEN

JASON HAD BOUGHT a kitchen stepladder in the hardware store in town. He dragged it to the broken stairs on the porch and set it up. What would it be like, seeing her after all these years?

Watching her drive away had broken him as a child. He'd worked hard to overcome that weakness, but he couldn't help wondering what her intentions now might be. He didn't let himself dwell on it. He'd show her the house and find out whether she'd been following Fleming.

Minutes later, sitting on the edge of the not-so-safe porch, he watched a battered, sun-bleached navy blue sedan struggle up the ragged driveway.

The woman behind the wheel parked and got out. He might not have known her if they hadn't scheduled the meeting. No wonder no one else in town recognized her.

She was just as Fleming had described, though more tired-looking than he'd imagined. She gazed at him with sad eyes that made him feel guilty, even though he hadn't been the one to wrong her. He had plenty of reasons to want his own payback.

In that moment of realization, all his old memories came flooding back. When she'd been younger and full of life, versus worn and anxious, she'd been his favorite person. He remembered her voice reading the books he'd later read to his siblings. Her hands, slender, unlined, unmarked, making a peanut butter sandwich, his favorite, with cherry preserves. He remembered her sweet, comforting smile.

Which he'd probably never see again because she eyed him warily, as if somehow he was responsible for wiping that kind of smile out of her repertoire.

"Jason?" Her trembling tone floated across the long weeds and brown grass, which was starting to look lacy as snow covered the mess.

He couldn't speak. He had missed her desperately as a child, but he didn't know her. He only knew she hadn't wanted him.

She acted now as if she were afraid someone would see her talking to him. She looked around as if she expected some sort of security detail to drag her off the property.

"I don't know what to call you," he said. She'd walked out on him. "Mom" wouldn't do.

"Can't call me Mother?"

"That's not what you are to me." He climbed to his feet. "Can you make it up the steps?"

"What am I, if not your mother?"

"The woman who gave birth to me."

She stopped and her face froze. "You've learned well at your father's feet."

"Let's not talk about him. I remember your arguments with each other. We don't need to recap."

"Why did you ask me here if you don't want to see me?" she asked.

"I was curious. Do you remember the last time we saw each other?"

"That morning when your father threw me out? How could I forget?"

"That's not the way I remember it. I remember begging you to stay, but you didn't seem to hear me. It was a like a bad dream. Trying to reach you, but you wouldn't even see me."

"I don't remember that," she said with perfect sincerity.

Jason resisted his own bewildered shock. He wouldn't ask her why again. Probably because the guy, Bryce, had distracted her. Even now, she refused to admit she hadn't been a good mother.

"Give me your hand. I'll help you up so you can see the house."

"I'm told you've owned it pretty much since the day I left."

"I didn't know until you called. It's all but derelict."

"So I'm noticing." She took his hand.

He stared at her. For the first time in over two decades, he was touching his mother. And she was a stranger. She'd chosen to be. "It's not much better on the inside, I'm afraid. I'm surprised you never took a look."

"I haven't been inside since it was taken away from me. I figured your father might have me arrested for trespassing if he found out I'd been here."

When she was steady on the porch, Jason let her go. She tried the sturdiness of the boards, bouncing on the balls of her feet a couple times.

"You make it sound like you're the victim," he said. "I don't understand that. You abandoned us and we never heard from you again. Ever."

She turned at the doorway. "What are you talking about?"

"You've heard of visitation?" he asked, easing past her into the dusty, abandoned home. He watched her face as she came in.

Sadness. It couldn't have been an act. Her eyes seemed to float in tears.

"Why did he do this?" she asked, as if she were alone and Jason not within earshot.

"Who?" But he knew. He just didn't understand her.

"Your father, of course. How could he let our home die?"

Their home? As if that meant anything to her. Jason went to the nearest window and stared through the broken panes. His father had made sure the home would die.

"You left with another man," Jason said, exasperated. "You didn't want to be with Dad or me. He must have known this house was the only thing that mattered enough to hurt you."

"That's enough, Jason. I can't believe you

accept that. Have you never learned how your father lies to suit his needs?"

His dad had colored more than one truth. "The kitchen's here." Jason led her down the hall. "What did he lie about?"

"Me." She stopped in the doorway, and he saw the kitchen through her eyes, the hole where the sink should be, the hanging wires and missing fixtures, the absence of hardware on the cabinetry. Tears fell freely down her face. "He lied about me. I begged him to let me take you with me. Then I begged him to let me visit you. After I tried to see you at your school, he had a restraining order applied."

Jason didn't want to believe her, but he felt as if someone had punched him so hard in the gut he couldn't breathe. "How could he do that?"

"I explained to the headmistress that I was only trying to see you, but she said the school couldn't get involved in domestic matters, and that because I hadn't been authorized as one of your caregivers, my presence was considered a threat to the children."

"Imagine that. A woman lurking outside a school's gates. A threat to the children." He didn't know whether to be angry with his father or let his impatience with her explode.

"My ex-husband lied to keep me away from the son I loved with all my heart. I made horrible mistakes when I was so lonely I went a little crazy, but I just wanted to see you. I needed to know you were all right after what I'd done. Did he drive you to school? Did he make your lunches? Did he show interest at all?"

"Dad was busy, but my grandparents did all those things."

"Busy? He was icy and disinterested—that's what sent me into another man's arms in the first place."

"So he made you cheat on him, is that it?" Jason couldn't accept her story. "Have you been hanging around outside a shop in town called Mainly Merry Christmas?"

She looked shaken, but nodded. "I shouldn't have, but I hoped to see you, that maybe we could talk if you saw me. I heard you spend time there with that pretty redhead. You don't answer my letters. Do you know how long it took me to get up the courage to ask you to see me?"

"Why didn't you get in touch when I was

in high school? My father wasn't in charge of me then."

"I tried, so many times. If you're saying you never heard from me, then your grandparents must have been intercepting my letters. They're good people, but they've always believed anything your father told them."

"You've heard of email?"

"I can't afford a computer. I have the most basic phone because it's cheaper than a landline. I have a menial job, and a little house with rent I can barely cover."

"Are you still trying to manipulate me? Do you think I'll hand this place back to you? Maybe after I renovate it? A little gift for my long-lost mother?" He walked toward the front door. "I have more reason to doubt you than my father. If I had a child, I'd turn the world upside down before I let anyone keep me away from him. So you're telling me you made a few efforts, but I've been an adult for how many years, and you didn't get in touch?"

She probably didn't even remember how old he was.

"I was shocked when I saw you in town. I thought you were your father coming out of the bank, and then I realized he couldn't look like that anymore." She touched her hair, which was as dry as straw. "I've certainly changed."

"Your looks have changed. Your story still doesn't convince me. You left my father for someone else because you were so starved for love?" Those were the words she'd shouted at his dad.

"That hasn't changed. The man I cheated with cheated on me, and I searched for the next guy who'd make me feel special. Over time I realized there was no such man. And this is who I am now."

"I don't know what game you're playing, and I'm not sure what it is you want," Jason said. "Even if you're telling the truth, you haven't given me a good reason for abandoning me."

He went to the front door, but only so he could turn his back so she couldn't see his face. His mother's broken spirit was a shroud around her shoulders. He'd meant to throw her out, but her story repeated itself in his head, and he experienced his first real doubts.

"Stay away from Fleming Harris and her store."

"GOOD NIGHT, MISS FLEMING," called the children in a ragged chorus as they sifted toward the exit, with moms and dads helping them into coats and gloves and scarves.

Fleming held the door open for the little ones, letting in the cold, Christmassy night air. She tugged a cap into place here, a coat sleeve down a bare wrist there. The moms nodded at her. The dads did likewise. The children each took a lollipop or a candy cane from the bowl in her hand.

She'd never liked peppermint so she'd never been a big fan of candy canes. Until cherry ones came along. But she provided both for the children who'd come in to paint ceramic mugs today.

After the last family trickled out, Fleming consulted her watch. She'd put in a good, hard day. She'd sold more ornaments and gewgaws than she'd hoped to because the parents had been happy to browse while she helped the children with their paints.

With Christmas getting closer and closer, sales were up, and so were Fleming's hopes.

She felt like she'd earned a break. She reached for the sign that said Open on one side and Closed on the other, tempted to turn it over and get in a few peaceful hours of writing on her own. She could just turn off the main lights and sit in front of her laptop at her makeshift desk, a table laden with wrapping paper and bows and all sizes of gift boxes.

But it was early enough that she might yet make another sale or two. Enough to help pay for the power and heat to keep the building open, come the new year. With the pragmatic thought came her sense of responsibility.

She left the sign on its Open side. Then she went to the back room and scooped up her laptop, unplugging it as she went, and set it on the counter up front. Bathed in warm light, with a living holiday image outside the wide, crystal-clear front windows, she perched on a stool.

She was available to anyone who needed last minute Christmas-themed goodies or a paint-it-yourself ceramic mug or papier-mâché ornament.

The first words came slowly. She saw her heroine, but was more aware of her paint-stained fingers on the keyboard. Her clicking keys echoed in the empty shop. She kept her fingers moving, and then somehow she forgot about the store and the windows and even customers.

She focused on the characters speaking in her head and the cool island breezes blowing across the beach in her story, and the emotions of her heroine, starting a brand-new life in a place she'd longed to be.

"Fleming?"

She looked up, as startled as if she were waking from a dream. Jason, in his usual perfect suit and overcoat, was standing in front of the counter. Only his tie was askew.

"Rough day?" she asked, closing the laptop, careful to look casual in an effort to make sure he didn't realize what she'd been up to. Her writing was a secret she'd never shared with another living being.

"What were you doing?"

He was too observant.

"Just work. Checking those spreadsheets," she said.

"I came inside and got all the way here to the counter without you noticing I was around. You didn't even hear the bells ringing over the door."

"Spreadsheets are important," she said. "I'm trying to keep the place open."

He stared at her, clearly considering. "I know we're not best friends, and my judgment might be off, but why are you lying to me?"

An odd jolt of guilt shook her resolve, but this was different. This secret was that dream Jason seemed to sense when no one else ever had.

She was afraid of bursting the delicate bubble if she shared her dream with anyone.

"Calling me a liar isn't very nice." She stood and walked around the counter, putting distance between herself and her secret. "Did you need something?" She waved her hands toward the shelves and flickering lights. "Something for your family back home?" Mention of his siblings and the father who was a clear source of combined pride and frustration always put Jason off his stride.

"You can trust me, you know."

She doubted. She always doubted first and, maybe, trusted later. "There's nothing."

He straightened his tie with the air of a man adjusting his armor. "I spoke to my mother. I told her to stay away from you."

"It was your mother?" He said it so easily, as if it weren't earth-shattering, as if he shouldn't be broken and bewildered by a mother who'd abandoned him, only to pop up years later out of the blue as if running away didn't matter. "Sit down. Let me get you some kind of a drink. I have cookies. Tell me what she said."

"No." He spoke so sharply Fleming backed up. He flinched. "I don't want to talk about what she said."

"She hurt you." Fleming was angry on his behalf. How dare the woman cause him more pain?

"Her story is a lot different from my father's." His grimace looked somehow rueful. "I just can't see why she bothered, but you don't need to worry about her anymore."

"What do you mean? You gave her the house?"

"No, I showed it to her, though. That's when she gave me a song and dance about having tried to reach me."

"Maybe she did try." Fleming wanted to believe that, for his sake, but he had a phone, an office, an address—he didn't seem like a difficult person to track down.

He seemed to read the doubt in her mind.

"Not hard enough." He glanced around. "How are things going?"

"Fine. Lots of business this week. I've been so busy I think we might be safe until February." What if he asked to see the books? She flicked a glance at the big clock on the back wall above the counter. "Time to close. I should be putting things away. Thanks for coming by." She walked him to the door. "Good night."

He nodded. "'Night."

She shut the door, but couldn't make herself look away as he pulled up the lapels of his coat and walked into the biting wind. She'd hardly been gracious, but what if he'd insisted on knowing what had kept her so intent on the computer?

She should have asked if there was anything she could do for him.

Other than show him the work she'd been doing on her laptop. "Close call," she said. She shouldn't feel bad about hiding her secret from a man who insisted she had no place in his life.

She leaned against the window, watching the snow sparkle and the looped strings of lights waver in the wind. The cold from the glass bit into her forehead as she strained to see Jason, hunched in his coat, striding away from her.

She wished she'd given more thought to his pain than to protecting her secrets.

## CHAPTER FOURTEEN

"Where's Jason tonight?"

Fleming didn't realize the question was directed her way.

"Fleming?"

She looked up. The carolers were all gathered on the square, but Mary Kite, who owned the oil and lube shop at the edge of town, must think Fleming had a hotline to Jason's activities. That wasn't so good. Imagine if Jason thought people were turning them into a couple. Not just his mother, or the nebulous possibility of someone, but a real live lube shop owner.

"I don't know." She knew she was the woman most likely to blush in the world, but with any luck the darkness offered her a shield. "Maybe he had to work late. I probably should have been doing that myself."

"Yeah, you and about three or four others of us." Mary turned her wrist over to check the time on her watch. "I'm one of the files on Jason's piled-high desk, too."

"You?" The group seemed to be taking an impromptu break, as their leader engaged in a hot and heavy discussion with the high school's music director. They often disagreed. "I would have thought everybody needed their car lubed."

"You would think that, but a chain in Sevierville has been offering a deal for the past year. A good deal. I can't match their prices, and I hear a lot of local people have made the drive. They get in a little shopping and have their car serviced all at the same time."

"But how do they shop without a car?"

"It's one of those quick places. You drive over the well and stay in the car while they do the oil change."

"Oh, no."

"Yeah. I can't expect to beat them for price or convenience. Not without another loan to build myself a handy well."

Fleming felt her pain. "It's hard, when you don't know what to do next."

"Maybe Jason will have some ideas for you," Mary said.

She didn't mean it in a snide way. Fleming knew that. But Mary's words felt like a well-aimed knife as she turned back to the group, who had finally agreed on the song they would sing next.

Fleming did likewise, and joined her voice with the others, but tonight she didn't have as much as fun as usual. She wandered with the others around the square, singing and laughing when required, but in her head, she kept hearing Mary's hopeful suggestion that Jason could help her store out of its troubles.

And she missed him.

She hated admitting it, but the night was not as fun because Jason never showed up.

She didn't want to face him with so many unsettling thoughts no doubt clearly printed on her face, but she wondered what had kept him. She wished again that she'd found a way to be more helpful with his mother and the strange story she'd given him.

After they finished practice, Mary suggested everyone join up for coffee.

"Thanks," Fleming said, "but I have to pick up today's mail, and I have a few tasks to do in the shop."

The other carolers waved goodbye. Fleming hurried toward the post office, which sat behind the square on a little side road. Folks who had a postal box were also provided with keys that opened the box area any time of the day or night.

Fleming let herself in and picked up the mail. But as she turned to leave, she saw Jason walking up with his key in his hand, side by side with Amanda Brent, who ran the dry cleaner's next door to his hotel.

Fleming almost laughed at the sudden surge of jealousy that caught her by surprise. As if Jason was her friend only. As if he couldn't hang out with other women in Bliss.

She was having a ridiculous night. She'd grown far too invested in Jason. She had to put an end to this. She didn't want to be the town laughingstock, pining for the bank's leg-breaker who might eventually foreclose on her.

"Evening," she said, as she opened the door for the two of them.

"Hey," Jason said. "I missed practice tonight."

"How did the carolers persuade you to join them?" Amanda asked, laughing up at him with the glow of a woman who was attracted.

Fleming took a deep breath. It bothered

her, but she didn't want that. She'd thought they could be friends. She might feel more than friendship, but she could control it, and she'd be all right when he left for his next job.

"I got swept into this singing thing," Jason said, with a meaningful glance at Fleming. "I didn't have a choice, and if you could hear me singing, you'd know that the group made a mistake."

"It's just for fun, though," Amanda said. "If you finish up on Christmas Eve outside the pub, you may get invited inside for some buttered rum or an Irish coffee. You can't go wrong."

"Why don't you sing with them?" Jason asked.

"No one ever asked me."

"You should come," Fleming said. "We've picked up new members every night we practice."

"Good idea," Jason said. "When's the next practice?"

"We were talking about the night after tomorrow. The group is having coffee right now. You guys should go over there and talk to them to make sure."

"Maybe we will," Amanda said. "Why don't you come along, Fleming?"

"Thanks, but I have some work to do at the shop." And she wanted to get out of here. No wonder she spent so much time alone. She didn't seem to handle adult relationships with aplomb. "Good night."

"See you soon," Amanda said.

Jason just smiled at her with a hint of confusion. She didn't blame him. She confused herself.

She tucked her mail under her arm and headed back to the store, letting herself in the back way. She sorted the bills and orders from the flyers and offers, and a note about taxes on the property. At least that was no surprise.

She got herself a mug of cocoa. This was more like it, getting her work done. Not thinking about Jason, who'd come to town for business and was determined to leave as soon as the job ended. He wasn't going to fall in love with the charm of Bliss. He wouldn't find that his hometown was the place he was supposed to be.

And he wasn't falling for her. His past intrigued her. His thoughts and feelings mattered to her. But in his estimation, she was probably just a friendly woman who didn't know her boundaries. In a town too small to hold him.

She had her own business to take care of. The shelves needed a good tidying. People moved things from here to there and just set unwanted items where they happened to be standing when they changed their minds. Fleming started at the front of the store, arranging shelves until she felt justified in taking a look at her writing.

She went to the counter and pulled out her laptop. First, she checked her email.

Her heart gave a leap when she saw the name of the mystery magazine to which she'd submitted a short story. Could it be a sale? Or would they call, in that case? She opened the email, closing her eyes as she clicked on the link.

There was only one way to find out. She opened one eye.

Big mistake on a night when she was already a touch out of sorts.

"Dear author" was never a good beginning, and the rest followed with even more discouraging news. They got the title wrong, but the "disappointing" characters had her characters' names. It was her story, all right, and they didn't want it.

She'd hoped. Man, how she'd hoped. She put her head down and breathed hard to keep from crying.

She rubbed at her eyes, but then looked at her screen again, and tears began to flow. It wasn't that she didn't love the shop. She wanted desperately to keep it alive and in her family. But she wanted this, too. This writing. It was impossible to be objective about it because it meant so much to her.

A sharp rap at the shop door rattled her. Shaking her head, she dashed a hand at the ridiculous, shaming tears, knowing before she looked that her caller would be Jason. He always showed up when she least expected him.

She found a smile and waved at him.

*Go away.* She willed him to leave, and tried even harder to smile in a way that would keep him from guessing she'd been weeping. This letter from the magazine—it was a rejection he wouldn't understand. But one that wouldn't stop her from trying again.

He opened the door and came inside.

"What's wrong?" he asked.

"Nothing." She closed the laptop and pushed her stool back. "I'm fine. What happened with you? I didn't expect to see you around here tonight."

"I was walking back to the hotel and I saw you." He came closer. "Go ahead and tell me it's none of my business if you want to, but I can see that you were crying. Don't pretend you weren't. My mother didn't show up here again, did she?"

Fleming tried to form the words. They wouldn't come. "I can't tell you it's none of your business."

"She was here? I can't believe it." He looked taken aback, and Fleming panicked.

If it felt like his business when she cried, what did that mean about their relationship? Or her inability to keep her own heart safe? "No, she wasn't. What I mean is that I can't be that rude to you."

He came around the counter. "You're not being rude if you just tell me you need comfort. What's got you crying in an empty store all alone a couple of weeks before Christmas?"

"That makes me sound pretty pathetic." The excitement and trouble she'd faced since

Thanksgiving suddenly piled up, making her feel pathetic, too. Tears seeped around all her best intentions, and she leaned forward, coming to rest on Jason's strong, broad chest.

He wrapped her in the warmth of his arms and dropped his chin on her head. She managed not to sob, but couldn't seem to stop the slow, steady drip of sadness. Too much had happened. She felt drained, of resourcefulness, of energy, of control.

Until she remembered she was weeping on her banker's expensive coat. Imagine the dry cleaning bill. Maybe Amanda offered him special rates.

Fleming straightened, forcing herself to fight for her missing control. She wiped her tears away once and for all and tried to look like a businesswoman, rather than a blotched, deeply disappointed damsel in distress.

"Thanks," she said. "I'm sorry for the way I'm behaving. I can't explain it."

"You mean you won't?"

She ignored the question. "I hope your coat won't have salt stains."

"Fleming?"

She glanced at him, but not for long. His gaze interrogated her. "I'm fine."

"Is it your mother? Hugh?"

"They're both fine. It's really nothing. Everything's fine."

"You can tell me if you want."

"And what will you do if I talk to you about something that bothers me this much? You can't fix it. I don't know how to fix it." That sounded as if she were giving up. She never would. Writing made her happy and whole, like nothing else. "But I'll figure it out, eventually."

"Okay." He ran his hand down her sleeve, and she didn't know what to say.

"Thank you," she said.

He laughed, a sweet, almost irresistible sound. She could be addicted if she let herself.

"For what?" he asked.

"For being kind when I needed kindness." She glanced back at her laptop, shut now, and innocuous looking. "Can I offer you some coffee or hot chocolate? Tea? I might have a beer back there."

"No, thanks. I'm on my way. I have a late meeting tonight."

He'd stopped only because she'd been upset. She couldn't contemplate what that meant without putting too much meaning into it. She had to get the truth straight in her head. They'd become friends, and he was only doing what a friend would do.

"Good night, Jason."

"I'll see you soon."

SNOWFLAKES AND ICE pellets floated out of the dark. Jason ran up the courthouse steps and stopped at a sign in the rotunda to search for the mayor's office. He ran his finger over the directory map and then memorized the way before he went to the nearest elevator.

The mayor's assistant had long since gone home for the night. A tidy desk sat outside double doors that opened into an ornate office that was being dominated by men's voices.

Surely there were women on Bliss's city council. Maybe Katherine should come home and run for office.

Jason knocked on the door frame. Five men and two women turned around. One man, the most prosperous looking, in a bespoke suit that silently proclaimed his success in life, came toward Jason, his hand outstretched.

"Jason, I'm Mayor Bradford. Nice to meet you."

"Mayor." Jason shook his hand. He glanced at the women and the rest of the men, who all looked him over as if they were searching him for something. "How can I help you? My father mentioned you might want to hear about the bank's progress."

"We've heard good things about the bank in the weeks since you've been here." Mayor Bradford gestured toward a chair, offering Jason a seat. "But we don't need to talk about the bank tonight."

Jason sat, intrigued. "I don't understand."

"We've asked you to meet us at this late hour for a specific reason. This man, Andy Steiger." The mayor gestured toward the guy at the end of the table. "He's leaving the council. He has a family matter that requires his attention, and he's resigning. We like the work you've done. We've looked into your résumé, and we feel you'd be good for business in Bliss. Your family has a long history here. Perhaps it's time you took your place back in our town. How would you like to replace Mr. Steiger?"

Jason stared at the group, who clearly felt they were bestowing an honor. They were, but it wasn't the role for him. It was for a man who didn't get itchy feet, who didn't need new challenges to conquer that he'd never found in a nine-to-five job for any extended length of time.

"I appreciate the opportunity," he said, "but I don't think I could commit to that kind of time. My work takes me all over the world."

"We understand you're renovating your father's former home here."

"I've been looking at it. Thinking about it." That was ridiculous and he knew it. He'd stopped fooling around in the wreckage and started phoning contractors. He seriously wanted to rebuild the place. It belonged in his family. His siblings might like to visit. His grandparents might want to spend time back in the mountain town that had been their first home.

And there was his mother...

"I remember when your father was a boy," an older man said, his voice gruff. "He had his ambitions. More than your grandfather or his father before him. Your dad was never going to stay in Bliss. He had his sights set on taller heights. I guess you take after him?"

Not a chance. If he had a family, Jason would stay put and take care of them. He wouldn't leave it to grandparents and older siblings. "I like my job. I do it well," he said. "But doing it means I have to travel."

There was silence. The rest of the council looked toward the mayor, who seemed to be thinking over his options.

"We don't expect you to give us your final answer right now," he finally said. "Naturally, you'd like to consider the possibilities. These fine people have discussed this matter thoroughly this evening, and I'm comfortable with our decision. Perhaps you and I could meet for lunch and discuss any issues you might have. You know, it's not a full-time job, but it would require a commitment. Take some time to think about what that might mean for you."

Jason almost said no. But these people might help or hinder his father's bank after he left town. And he owed them the courtesy of considering their offer.

"Don't you have local people who could take Mr. Steiger's seat?"

"We like the way you work." Mayor Bradley seemed to be pretending he hadn't heard a word Jason had said. At best, he hadn't listened.

"I'll get in touch with you tomorrow about lunch." Jason stood and nodded at the group around the table. "Thanks for asking me up here. I appreciate your considering me for such an important position."

"You have skills we need in this town. More homegrown business, less reliant on tourism, would be a huge plus for us. You obviously know how to build and repair a company."

Jason wasn't sure they could know so much about him simply because his family's bank was getting itself in order. They'd obviously done some research. He nodded and shook each hand offered to him before he left.

The idea surprised him, and challenged him a bit. What would it be like to restore his family's home and work in this town where he'd been born? The council might welcome him, but how would he be accepted by the people whose homes and businesses were dependent on the measures he'd taken?

Like Fleming?

He reached for the door handle. What really stood between them except his wandering feet and her inexplicable affection for this town buried in the woods and mountains of Tennessee?

Who was he kidding? He was unwilling to commit to any relationship. When he cared enough for a woman, maybe that commitment would come.

When he thought of Fleming, his yearning for her unnerved him. He wanted to believe she could be in his life. But even if she wanted him, could he stay? He never had before.

No one ever stayed.

# CHAPTER FIFTEEN

AT LAST THE ornaments had arrived. The ones they offered at Mainly Merry Christmas each holiday season, special to Bliss, marked with the year and the place. Fleming loved the ornaments. But more importantly, they brought in sales. Many people in town collected them, and many bought them as gifts for their children or parents or friends who'd moved away.

Just over a week before Christmas, Fleming unpacked the ornaments and hung them on a tree she put up by the counter.

Then she set up a sandwich-board sign. With red and green chalk and her best penmanship, she announced the arrival of this year's collectible ornament, and drew Christmas trees, Santas, sleighs and snowmen.

She carried the sign out to the sunny sidewalk, where she realized she had to tidy up some of her chalk drawings. Art was clearly not her thing. The Santas looked a little more

Halloween than Christmas—which couldn't be good for business.

She heard the clicking of high-heeled boots on the concrete before a voice spoke behind her. "You're friends with that banker, Jason Macland, aren't you, Fleming?"

Fleming almost fell onto the sign. She twisted to see who was speaking. Sue Bradford, the mayor's wife, in a thick wool coat and a cute hand-knitted cap, peered at her over shopping bags.

"Hi, Sue."

"I'm sorry, I didn't mean to startle you. My husband asked me to talk to you about Jason."

Fleming wished she could crawl away. The more she wanted to distance herself from Jason, the more people seemed to piece them together. She scrambled to her feet, dusting chalk off her jeans. "I don't really know him that well, Sue. He holds my mortgage."

"Yours and several others from what I hear."

"Uh-huh." Where was this going? "We're not that close or anything."

"No, but I see you with him quite often. You persuaded him to join the carolers?"

"Well, he is singing with us, but…"

"Okay." Sue adjusted her packages and saw the sign. "Oh, the new ornaments are in? Let's go inside. I need to get one for my sister in New Hampshire, and I need one, and I'm starting a collection for the children, too."

Cash register sounds cha-chinged in Fleming's imagination. She felt a little guilty, commercializing Christmas, but she was also glad of the sales. "Would you like something warm to drink, Sue? Tea?"

"Tea would be delightful. Or coffee if you have it."

Fleming had a commercial urn set up with holiday-spice coffee right now, giving the store an inviting scent. She held the door for Sue.

"Let me get you a cup. Put your bags anywhere."

She had mismatched cups and saucers in the back that she'd bought over the years in antiques stores. Pretty and delicate, they were a nice treat for browsers in the shop. She took a couple from the back and poured coffee for two. After adding a little cream to her own cup, she set Sue's by the urn.

In a moment, she'd set out a bowl of small,

wrapped chocolates and a plate of cookies in cellophane packages.

"Help yourself to sugar and cream and a bite to eat," she said.

"Thanks."

"How many ornaments? I'll package them up for you."

"Are you gift wrapping? That would be such a relief."

"Sure."

"Good. I'll take seven. Then I'll have a few extra in case I need them. My husband likes to send them out to friends in the capital."

Everyone in Bliss assumed Mayor Bradford had his sights set on Nashville and beyond.

"I'll get them from the back. The ones still in their boxes will be easier to wrap."

"I can't stand to do the wrapping every year," Sue said. "I love shopping, and I really enjoy watching my friends and family opening their gifts, but if someone would come home with me and wrap everything the night before Christmas, I'd believe in Santa and all his elves again."

Fleming laughed, but it was another idea to keep in mind in case she needed a job next year.

Balancing her coffee cup and saucer, Sue perched herself on a stool in front of the wrapping station. She was sipping coffee and swinging her legs like a happy child when Fleming brought the ornaments out.

"Tell me about this Jason." Sue reached out to one of the tubes of paper. "I like this one with the bells."

"I don't know a lot about him," Fleming said. What she did know she didn't plan to spread as gossip. "He hasn't said anything about politics, if the mayor's worried about that."

Sue laughed. "I love that everyone in this town assumes my husband is always thinking how he's going to attain his next public office. He wants your banker to join the city council. He and the rest of the members spoke to Jason last night." She stopped, placing one finger over her mouth. "I wonder if I was supposed to say that to anyone? Well, you won't spread it around, will you?"

Fleming shook her head, trying to imagine what Jason, a successful consultant who'd made his reputation and living by moving job to job, state to state and even country to country, had said to the offer of a steady commitment in a place that clearly wasn't a happy memory for his family. "That's an easy promise to keep."

"Good. I knew I could count on you. Anyway, Tim has also noticed you spend a lot of time with Jason, and we both wondered if you might try to exert your influence. Maybe if he understood how much this town needs a go-getter like him…"

"He has a job, Sue. He likes to travel. I don't think he's interested in a position that would require him to stay put."

"See? You know his preferences. You're the perfect person to persuade him this could be a good deal. And it would round out his résumé."

"His résumé?" Fleming's hands stilled on the package she was wrapping. "You've read it? He applied for this appointment?"

Sue shook her head and glanced toward the shelves, flustered. "He didn't apply, but I have seen his CV. You'd be amazed at the things you can find online. My husband showed it to me when he asked me to speak to you."

"I have no influence with Jason."

Sue arched one eyebrow, but her attempt to

look knowing was more sweet than upsetting. "Everyone has seen the two of you together."

Fleming couldn't help laughing.

Sue smiled as well, but halfheartedly. "There's been talk, is what I'm trying to tell you."

"I got that. I'm not surprised that our good neighbors managed to work up the will to gossip, but they're off base with me."

"And Jason," Sue added.

"There is no Jason and me."

"But you'll speak to him?"

Fleming stared at the seven ornaments on the counter in front of her. "You're being more relentless than usual, Sue."

"I don't usually have to try so hard when I'm asking you to help with a toy drive or a knitting circle or the children's Halloween festival."

"You aren't trying to influence me by buying all these?"

"I'd buy seven more if that would work. Tim's being a bit relentless about this, as well. Jason got his start in banking, but Tim has seen what his work has done to save other companies, and he believes he can take on our community as if it were an ailing business."

"Do we need saving?"

"The council worries every time there's a dip in the tourism dollar. 'Banking is only one arrow in Jason Fleming's quiver.'" Sue rolled her eyes. "I'm quoting my husband. He said to tell you Jason wouldn't have to stay here year-round. He'd just have to commit to a certain number of hours, which they could negotiate."

"But wouldn't the council prefer someone who's committed to Bliss?"

"They want someone with his proven skills."

Fleming tried to keep the flicker of her own hope at a low burn, though it was battling to turn into a flame. "I'll suggest it's a good idea." It would give him more time to look into his own family's past. There must be people here who remembered the Maclands before they'd surfed the wave of banking wealth all the way to New York.

"That's all I can ask for," Sue said with relief. She reached for an ornament. "Pass me that paper. I'll help you with this."

"I thought you didn't like wrapping."

"I don't, but I didn't expect you to put up

such a fight, and now I'm concerned you'll want a favor of equal value in return."

Fleming passed the paper across. "Not sure that's possible."

AT FIRST, FLEMING thought she'd wait for Jason to come around again before she dared to ask him about the council position. Or, she could bring it up if she ran into him at carol practice, but she couldn't be sure he'd appear after missing last time.

But it weighed on her mind. She worried about coming across like his parents, as if she were trying to manipulate him.

Funny that going to his office required courage.

But it did. Because she wanted to see him. She liked the sound of his voice, and the warmth she sometimes saw in his eyes that made him seem as if he kind of liked her. She even liked that he made her look inside herself with his own troubling questions.

She dressed the morning after Mrs. Mayor's visit with more care than she normally put into choosing clothing. A little black dress, black tights, pumps and a white sweater looked cute, businesslike and comfortable.

But then she was running later than she wanted because she couldn't open the store until after she visited the bank. She hopped in the car and headed down the mountain.

The benefit of going into town early was bountiful parking and hardly any of her fellow citizens to comment on her visit.

She hurried through the lobby at the bank, her heels tapping for once as if she was a woman with places to go—or as if she was a woman on a mission to get in and out of the building as quickly as possible.

At the elevator, she punched Jason's floor number and sent up a silent thanks at being the car's only passenger. She stepped out into the reception area when the doors opened. No one was manning the desk, so she went to Jason's door and knocked.

"I've told you that you don't have to knock, Hilda," he said from inside.

Fleming opened the door and put her head inside the office. "I'm not Hilda. Do you have a minute?"

Jason dropped his pen and stood. "What are you doing here?"

"Is that like, 'Yes, come inside'?"

"That's exactly what it's like." He smiled,

but with the clear suspicion that she was up to something. "What's up?"

"What do you mean?" She hadn't expected a glowing welcome, but an indulgent glance might have been nice, at least.

"You don't drop by for visits."

"Except when I was working on ways to avoid losing my livelihood."

"Okay."

He was the man who might have made her homeless. Neither of them needed that reminder.

Fleming sat down in the chair in front of his desk, even though he hadn't asked her. Sitting would make this easier. She felt unnerved now. She didn't get the sense she was welcome in his office, so how was she supposed to be persuasive about asking him if he'd take the council job? Especially when it felt like none of her business.

Jason sat as well, and took up his pen again.

"Do you know Sue Bradford?" Fleming asked. No need to work up to it. She shouldn't have come, anyway.

"Sue?" he asked. "No, I don't think so—any relation to the mayor?"

"His wife. She stopped by my shop yester-

day, to buy a couple of this year's ornaments."
Rambling. That was always persuasive.
"While I was wrapping her purchases, she
mentioned that the mayor had suggested you
join the town council."

"And you came to tell me to stay out?"

Fleming blinked. His leap to the wrong
conclusion silenced her.

He tapped his pen on the desktop. "I already told him I didn't want the job. It
couldn't work with my travel schedule anyway, and I realize not everyone in this town
would see me as a good candidate."

"I was going to ask you to consider taking
it," Fleming said. "You don't give us enough
credit. I didn't realize Mr. Paige had given me
terms that wouldn't work. I didn't even realize the kind of trouble we were in. But all of
it was my fault, not yours. I may not like that
you're the one who had to give me the bad
news, but I'm grateful someone did before I
lost the store entirely."

Jason sat back. "You really feel that way?"

"I can't be the only one who's seen sense."

"You'd be surprised," he said. "I've had to
look into the faces of people in serious finan-

cial trouble. I doubt I've enjoyed it any more than they have."

"But now you know these people. You've tried to help all of us. That's what you'd be doing with the council, too. And Sue asked me to remind you that you only have to commit to a certain number of agreed-upon hours."

"If I were staying," he said. "But I'm not. I have another job lined up for the first of February, and they'd be happy to have me come earlier if I can make it." He glanced at his computer screen. "I think I can."

His simple statement had a painfully complicated effect on Fleming. She felt as if she'd been hit by something hard and shocking. Not one ounce of regret was evident in his face or in his tone. He was just moving on, as if no one here had any hold on him.

She hadn't realized she'd wanted to have a hold, or that not having one could hurt so much. She'd truly started to care for Jason Macland.

How could she have let that happen, knowing the kind of man he was? Not a bad man or a cruel one. But a guy who moved on.

This might be the lesson she needed to

learn in life. It wasn't the first time she'd realized she cared about something too late to do anything about it. She'd let her father go when she should have taken a chance on getting to know him. She'd let herself feel too much for Jason when she should have known he was just a friend.

He was only ever going to be just a friend.

"I have to go." She stood and turned with less poise than she would have liked. "The store is still closed. I have to pick up…some things…before I open it. You should think about the job," she said, hoping to mask her distress.

She'd had it wrong. He didn't care for her the way she wanted him to. She was in this alone.

"Thanks, Fleming."

"Sure," she said, without a backward glance.

"Maybe I'll stop by for one of those special ornaments."

"I'll send one over, if you'd like."

As if she was in the habit of hiring a courier for deliveries around the square. She just didn't want to see Jason Macland face-to-face again until she had herself under control.

## CHAPTER SIXTEEN

"GLAD TO SEE YOU, Fleming," Lyle Benjamin said. "Are you staying to enjoy our Sunday dinner special?"

She looked up. A week before Christmas the snow was falling in the blue blackness of the night outside the window behind Lyle's head. She lifted her sandwich. "You make the best pimento cheese in town. I just don't get how it's a holiday tradition."

As the sign outside on the sidewalk had proclaimed.

"It is in my family," he said. "My dad loved pimento cheese. We had it every day during Christmas vacation when he was home with my brothers and me."

Fleming nodded. "Makes sense." Every family had its traditions. Hers and her mother's had fallen apart since her graduation, but she wasn't a child any longer. It was more than time her mother began making traditions with Hugh.

And Fleming made her own.

"You don't come around much anymore. Did you and Jason have a falling out?"

"No," she said, in a knee-jerk reaction, hoping to quell that rumor before the hotel owner could spread it too far. "I don't have help at the store right now so I can't get away often." She looked at her sandwich for the perfect mouthful. A piece of cheddar was grilled into both sides, and the filling leaked out over her fingers with each bite. Combined with collard greens, it was a dinner fit for royalty, even if it didn't suggest Santa and decking the halls. "But I do love your traditional pimento."

"You know Jason's been working on that house of his."

Lyle looked at her as if he assumed she knew what he meant. She hesitated, but what the heck? "I didn't know he was talking about that place."

"You thought you were keeping a secret for him by not mentioning it? I enjoy that idea." It seemed Lyle had caught the matchmaking bug. "He borrowed some of my tools. He said he needed to repair the porch steps so that he and his contractor could enter the house safely."

"He's hired a contractor?"

"Owen Gage. The clinic he's been working on will be finished soon. Owen's done good work on that."

She almost asked what Jason planned to do with the house, but just in time remembered it was none of her business. Then she started to ask if he was rethinking the council's open seat, but she managed to quash that, too.

She should get out of here before she gave away everything she knew about Jason Macland. "I have to get going, Lyle. Thanks for a delicious dinner."

"Glad to see you back in my dining room again. Don't stay away. We business owners need to support each other in this town."

Wondering how long she'd remain one of the town's business owners, Fleming dug into her purse for money to pay her bill. She left it beside her plate as Lyle topped off coffee cups for the couple at the table next to hers.

"Say hello to Jason for me," Lyle said.

She stopped for a second, trying to come up with a fitting response. "Shh, someone will hear you" seemed a little paranoid, so she held that inside, too.

She hadn't seen Jason in several days. She'd even wondered if he might have gone. He had no obligation to tell her he was leaving, but she'd missed him.

She'd miss any friend she hadn't seen in a while. She wanted to know what was on his mind. They were close enough that they could talk about his plans without a conversation having to mean anything more intimate.

He came by her store all the time, and he'd even surprised her at home that one time. There was no reason she couldn't drop in on him.

"Lyle," she said, "I'll have one of your Christmas pimento cheese sandwich dinners to go."

"Coming right up."

She was soon on her way. Jason's car wasn't at the bank or in the hotel lot, but there was one other place she thought she might find him. She began to lose her nerve as she drove up the mountain. Until she turned onto Jason's road, she wasn't sure if she would manage to stop in or drive past.

After all, pimento cheese leftovers for her own lunch tomorrow would be no hardship.

But she wouldn't be eating those leftovers. She made the several sharp turns that led to the Macland property. As she parked behind Jason's car, she spied him by the light of lights hanging from his porch roof, banging away at fresh wood on newly framed steps. He straightened, a power hammer in one hand. He pressed the other hand into the small of his back.

She couldn't help smiling. When had he last done manual labor?

He turned toward her, but she couldn't read his expression. She suddenly wanted to stay in her car and drive home.

She didn't.

"I didn't expect you," he said, as she exited the driver's seat.

"What are you doing?"

He held up the nail gun. His work was sort of obvious. "Fixing the porch. You remember almost falling through?"

"But why, Jason?" She reached back into the car for the bag containing his sandwich and collard greens and a side of Parmesan fries. A true carb load. "You don't like it here," she said. "You don't want to stay."

"I never said I didn't like it here."

She wasn't willing to argue. The last thing she wanted was for him to see what she'd discovered in his office—that she cared what he decided about his future in Bliss.

Or his lack of a future here. That was the more likely possibility, and she needed to brace herself for it.

"I brought you dinner," she said. "Lyle's holiday special."

"That pimento cheese thing?" Jason shook his head. "I don't get it. A cheese sandwich as a special in the Christmas season."

"I asked him the same question. It was his father's favorite. Have you ever tried it?"

He shook his head again. "Not here. I had one when I went to the Masters in Augusta once."

"Fancy. I like golf. I'm terrible at it, but I like it. How did you get tickets to the Masters?"

"A client invited me."

She nodded. Clients here brought him collard greens and a sandwich. "I should have grabbed some paper plates."

He set down the nail gun and took the bag from her, but when he opened it, he looked surprised. "You didn't bring enough for both of us?"

"I already ate." She shivered, hunching her shoulders in the cold wind that whistled around the higher elevations. "I'm not sure why you're working out here in the dark, but should we try to find a spot inside?

"Sure." He helped her over the spaces between the safer steps. "We'll try the kitchen."

"You don't suppose there are any animals inside?" she asked, hanging back. "When I was a kid, my friends and I went into an abandoned house that used to be near the square. It's a yarn shop now. But when we were looking in the upstairs bedroom, a possum came slithering out from under the bed."

"A possum?"

"During the daylight. Of course, it might have been resting, but my mom always told me possums out in the daytime were probably rabid. We almost jumped through the windows, but the possum was quicker than we were, and it got out of the room and ran somewhere. We bolted from the house."

"I'm not sure whether to laugh at you or be offended that you call my house abandoned."

She picked her way across the porch. "My mom raised a petition to have the yarn shop house razed. Instead, someone bought it at a good price and opened a business."

He held the door for her. "I'm grateful I don't hold the mortgage on that one."

She couldn't help laughing at his heartfelt admission, but she also noticed the changes he'd made in the house. More of those lights were hanging in each room. "You've been sweeping." Dust motes still hung in the air.

"It was dirty. I wanted to see what the place looked like. Devoid of furnishings, of course. I figure your friends and neighbors came in and shopped for things at a really low price. My mother said my father left most of the furniture here when he moved out."

"I don't know anyone who would steal your family's belongings," she said.

"I wasn't accusing you." He pushed through the swinging kitchen door. "I was trying to make a joke. I swept in here last night. The leftover dust should be more settled."

He must also have righted the two wooden chairs by the Formica table no one had wanted as much as they'd wanted the sink. He grabbed a thermos and a cup off the counter.

"I'm glad you brought that," Fleming said. "I didn't think of a drink."

"Coffee." He poured some into the cup and pushed it to her. "I don't have cream or sugar."

"This is fine. Thanks. It'll be perfect in here."

"It is a little chilly." To punctuate his statement, a gust of wind rattled the wide windows on the kitchen wall above the sink.

"But it looks nicer." Fleming went to the counter. Butcher block, scarred, but obviously well-used. "Someone did love this place once."

"My mother, apparently."

"Are you going to give it back to her?"

He stared at Fleming as she turned to face him. She couldn't read his careful gaze. He finally shrugged. "I don't know what to do about that. Staying in one place doesn't seem to be her strong suit, either. I want it for my family, but I'm not sure my mother could afford the taxes, even. I haven't talked to her since I told her to stay away from you."

"You're feeling attached to the house?"

He sat, placing his thermos to one side. Then he ripped open the paper bag, spreading the plastic silverware, the container of greens and the box that held his sandwich and fries over the torn expanse of paper. "I don't know that I feel attached, either," he said. "Maybe intrigued."

"What are you planning to do here, Jason?" Fleming picked up the coffee cup he'd left on the counter and sat in the chair opposite his.

"Why do you want to know?"

His bluntness took her aback. "I thought I could ask you nosy questions without being questioned in return. I'm just surprised that you aren't planning to sell it."

"I can regret that my parents neglected the home that was mine, without wanting to live in a small town on top of a mountain."

Fleming felt as if he'd slapped her hands, like her mom had once when she'd almost touched the hot stove as a child. "Okay."

"Are you suggesting I should repair it for my mother?"

"Not my business," Fleming said brusquely, to cover her hurt feelings. She ran her fingers over the Formica. "I'm surprised no one took this. It would sell for quite a bit in one of those retro stores in town. Your mother, even—I'd have been tempted to take back my kitchen table if I wanted my house enough to ask my estranged son to find a way for me to live in it."

"You think people should just take the things they want?"

She flushed. In fact, her skin felt as if it were on fire. "Not at all. I'm an honest person even if I did get behind in mortgage payments."

"I didn't mean you weren't."

"Are you picking a fight?"

He opened the lid on his greens and peered at them. "Not on purpose. What's this?"

"Collard greens. You haven't had them before?"

"I can't be sure." He opened the plastic-wrapped cutlery and took out a fork to test the collards. "You like them?"

"I love them, and Lyle's are the best. Even better than my mother's."

"She's a good cook?"

"Really good."

"Except for your problems with your father, you had a pretty good childhood." He speared a bite of greens and tried them, looking surprised as he chewed with more gusto. "Hey—these are good."

"Wait until you try the sandwich. And it's even better when the cheese is still hot."

He picked it up. "It's warmish. Thanks for thinking of me." He took a bite and his smile made Fleming happy. He chewed with relish. "This is a work of art."

"Enjoy." It was always nice when someone enjoyed a gift you'd given them.

"Was I right? Did you have a pretty good childhood?" he asked again.

His doggedness startled her, but she thought before she answered. "I guess I did," she said. "Why?" What difference did it make to him? Why should he—

She got spooked. "Are you wondering how well I'll cope if you foreclose on the store? Do you think I'll fall apart and run away?"

She realized even as she spoke how ridiculous the question sounded. They were both feeling prickly with each other.

"Hold on," he said. "Your mind bobs and weaves in ways I can't follow. I'm not going to foreclose on the store. You're holding your own." He grimaced. "For now."

"For now?"

"I know it's only part of the picture, but some days your bank deposits are better than others."

"Are you keeping such a close eye on everyone's loan? Are you even allowed to look into our accounts?"

"I'm not normally so hands-on," he said. "But you make this business more personal. I don't want you to fail."

"Why did you want to know about my childhood?" She didn't want to go any more deeply into the concept of her business being personal to him. He was leaving. She would stay in Bliss all her life.

"I can't say, exactly." He took another bite of sandwich. "I guess I'm thinking more about my own past since I heard from my mother. I've asked my father why she insists she tried to get in touch, but he's ducking me."

"Why do you let him duck?"

"You see?" He leaned back. "You're emotional and happy and anxious, all at the same time, but you had a parent who didn't exactly stick around. I wonder what makes you so willing to feel, when I'm trying hard not to care."

"About what?" she asked, suddenly unable

to catch her breath. She'd heard the expression "heart in your throat," but she'd never considered what that must feel like until this moment.

"I don't even know," he said. "Well, yes, I do. I don't want to care about what happened in the past. I do care about what happens to your business, and I care what happens to my mother. I don't like to think of her longing for this house, but unable to get home."

"Where is your home? Do you long for it?"

He nodded. "You know that moment when you walk through your own door, when you haven't been home in ages?"

"I felt that way coming back from college."

"You see? You're a part of Bliss. It's a part of you. I have to ask myself if my mother feels about this house the way you do about your town," Jason said. "I have an apartment with furniture a decorator chose and paintings I couldn't describe to you if you asked me, but it's home. I stay there between jobs, and I'm glad there's still a bookstore in the neighborhood with good Wi-Fi and even better coffee."

"You could be part of Bliss, too. People

want you here." She felt as if she were choking. People. Sure. "The mayor, the council."

Jason stared at her, his eyes expressionless. She wished she could call back the words. He nodded.

"I could put down roots anywhere, I suppose, but Bliss is hardly handy for travel," he said.

"And you have to travel?"

"I enjoy my work. Like you enjoy yours." He passed her a french fry. "Did you try one of these?"

"They were my favorite after-school snack when I was in high school. My mother doesn't know that. Unless Lyle ratted me out." She laughed. "There are advantages to not living in a town where everyone is willing to share your worst secrets with your parents."

"Neighborhoods can be like that in New York. Not mine. People come and go too frequently. I'm not sure anyone there considers the option of putting down roots. We're all on the way somewhere. If not to a new job, to a new neighborhood, with a higher price tag or a more prestigious address."

"We have those here, too, but most people

live in them part-time. A lot of the wealthier homeowners here are only on vacation."

He lifted both brows, his gaze reflective. "Not even my father feels the need for a vacation home he might use for only a few weeks a year."

"I assumed everyone who lived in New York had second homes." She grinned. "From watching reality shows on TV."

"I don't see you as a reality-show fan."

"Sometimes when I'm working, I leave it on for company. Background noise."

Too late, she realized her slip.

"Background noise while you work?" he asked. "I don't remember a television in the store."

She looked around the kitchen as if she'd never seen anything that mattered to her as much. "What are you doing next? Do you want me to find some polish for these counters?"

He stared at her. "What? Where would you find polish in this house? Why would I want the counters polished when I'm not even sure the floors aren't about to fall in?"

She stared back. "I've gone blank."

"Blank." He looked at her as if he was seeing new parts of her he hadn't expected. "So am I. What's going on with you? What are you trying to hide?"

"I'm not hiding anything."

"You're one of the worst liars I've ever met, and you know I see a few of them in my line of work."

"People lie to their bankers?"

"Not just to a banker. Business owners lie to me about the state of their accounts and their prospects. They lie about mistakes they've made in the past, and you've been lying from the first day I met you about something that matters to you as much as the shop."

"I don't understand why you think that."

"Because it's four walls and objects. You make it pretty, but it doesn't challenge you. You think too much to be completely satisfied by sales figures."

She opened her mouth, but words wouldn't come. If she confessed her writing dreams, how foolish would she feel? She was spending all this time on work that didn't pay, on hopes that might never come to fruition.

A business consultant, whose bottom line was profit, would never understand. He'd be even more frustrated with her, and she didn't want that to matter. She didn't want to make him believe he was taking a risk on a bad loan with her, but more than that, his opinion of her counted.

"What is it? Where do you work with a television? Have you taken some part-time job in a call center or something?"

"Do they leave televisions on?"

"Fleming, I don't understand you."

His determination touched her. He wanted to save her from a second job that hardly paid. Imagine what he'd think of the gut-sucking pain of being rejected for work that so far hadn't paid anything at all?

"You don't have the right to understand me. We don't matter to each other."

"You know that's not true. You do matter."

"I'm repeating what you've said over and over. If I have a secret, I'm not sure why I'd tell you when I haven't told my friends or my mother, or anyone else in this whole wide world."

Jason looked at her as if he could will her to spill her story. "I can't imagine what you're hiding. How bad could it be?"

"It's not bad." She stared at her hands on

the table. At the fingers that often ached from typing. Her thumb that cramped from repeatedly pressing the space bar.

Jason took another bite of his sandwich. "You don't have to tell me. As long as it doesn't affect what you do in the store, you're correct. I don't really have any right to ask."

And just like that, she wanted to tell him, because he no longer cared enough to ask again. She wanted to share the hope that was a light inside her when she felt dark about the store and the future.

"I write," she said. "I've submitted stories here and there. Short ones, novellas, a longer novel."

He sat back. "That's what you're doing at your laptop when I pass the store at night and you're buried in something on that screen. I thought it was your spreadsheets."

"How many times have you walked by? I've only noticed you once."

"Because you're steeped in the stories you're writing. That's your passion."

She couldn't deny it. "Don't start on me about giving up Mom's store. My store," she said, already regretting her moment of truth.

"You haven't sold any of your stories?"

Her ego, almost always in a state of being bruised about her writing, seemed to melt away like a piece of ice in the sun. "How did you know?"

"I'd assume you'd talk about it if you had something published."

"I guess I would."

"You'd have to. Promotion," he said.

"You're a businessman, first and foremost," she said. "Don't you love something in your life so much you can't be pragmatic about it?"

His quick glance around the kitchen startled her.

"Could you love this house like that, Jason?"

He didn't answer. Apparently, he had something to hide, too. An ability to care about this house. Maybe about his family. Maybe about more.

Or maybe he didn't know what it felt like to love that much. Maybe he never would.

"I feel connected to this place." He took the last mouthful of his sandwich and licked a smidgen of pimento cheese from the pad of his thumb. "I don't know why, and I'm not sure I want to be connected, but it was my home, and I think I can feel that to be true."

"I really don't understand your family."

Looking up, Fleming noticed only a few squares of tin were left on the ceiling. And they were so dented they might have been left because the neighborhood looters hadn't thought them worthy of stealing. "How do you just walk away?"

"From your children and your home? No idea." Jason wadded up his sandwich wrapper and tucked the last few fries into the torn brown paper.

"My mom couldn't bring herself to leave here even when the man she loved lived almost two hours away."

"And now you're returning the favor she did you." Jason lifted the container of collards and stabbed the last few leaves with his fork. "You're putting her dreams before yours like she put your happiness first."

"You need to believe me about the shop. It's my future, too. I can't count on selling my work, and I have to support myself. This year, when I'm all but begging people to buy, I realize how I'd miss the holidays if I didn't have the shop. It wouldn't feel normal."

"Why haven't you told your mother about your writing?" he asked, putting the lid back on the empty container.

"I'm not even sure why I told you." She stood and tucked her chair back beneath the table as if this were someone's well-loved home.

"I'm glad you did."

She braced herself. "Will my alternate plan make you feel a little better about taking the store if I can't make it profitable? You must not have grasped the part where I have yet to be paid for anything I've written."

He shook his head, pushing his own chair back. "Thanks for also sharing your high opinion of me. I'm glad you told me the truth. I knew there was something you loved to do. There had to be something other than the store."

"I do love writing." She walked ahead of him to the kitchen door, pausing to push a dangling piece of rooster-emblazoned wallpaper back against the plaster. "What do you love?"

"What kind of work?" He sounded surprised. "My job. I like making order out of chaos. Restoring a sick business to health. My skill is for seeing the big picture—like I could see you making a living at the work that makes you happy."

"I haven't been slacking at the shop," she said, hating that she felt defensive.

"I didn't say you had. You asked what I like to do as much as you like writing, and I told you, and then I extrapolated a scenario where you might also make a living at some work you find more rewarding than running Mainly Merry Christmas."

"No." She couldn't find words to argue with all that, so a simple no had to do. "And I don't want to discuss it. What do you want me to do while you rebuild those steps?"

"Help me," he said, without even an effort at putting her off. "I can't seem to hold the replacement wood in place and use the nail gun at the same time."

But when they got to the front door, he stopped and looked at her with fresh eyes again. "Fleming," he said. His concern startled her. She was even more startled when he pulled her into his arms.

"What's up with you?" she asked, breathing in his scent—of the woods, and smoke from someone's chimney that had drifted down the mountain and into his sweatshirt. His arms were strong and certain. His touch was kind, and yet confident. She wanted to relax against him, but self-preservation demanded she not fall for this handsome, thoughtful man.

He'd be leaving her behind soon.

"I just realized why you were crying that night in your store," he said. "You must have received a rejection."

And he cared enough to comfort her? She took a deep breath. It was comfort. Nothing more. *Keep it in perspective.*

She looked up at him, resting her hands against his sides, trying not to notice the softness of his sweatshirt, the heat of him underneath the worn material. "I've been rejected a few times," she said, trying to be pragmatic. But the pain came flooding back as she remembered the "interesting, but not strong enough" comment on the editor's notes. "Enough to paper the ladies' room at the shop, but that one—that story—I thought…"

Jason tucked her head beneath his chin. "I'm sorry," he said. "You have a spirit of joy about you, Fleming Harris. That must come through in your stories."

Her breath caught. She might be drowning in his warmth, and she didn't have anything to grab on to for safety. "I don't know about that," she said. "But thank you. I'm not sure anyone except my mom has ever looked at me and thought *joyful*."

"Then people in this town don't talk to each other. I can tell the folks around here like you."

Fleming realized she was still in his arms. She pulled away and eased herself out onto the porch. She'd really wanted to stay right where she was, next to Jason's beating heart. "What people? I'm not sure everyone is open with their feelings around you."

"At the coffee shop after that carol practice I missed, the others in the group asked about you as if we were supposed to show up together. They all hope there's more to our friendship than a shared interest in singing holiday songs."

Fleming wanted to sink into the house's exposed crawl space. "I really might cry again." She eased down the steps and struggled to set the next plank in place for him to nail. It was easier when he took the other end, and they settled it on its braces together. "I'm sorry about my neighbors assuming we're with each other. It's a small town. You're well-known because of the bank, and I've been here on the square all my life. Gossip is a pretty big industry around Bliss."

"I don't care as long as it doesn't make problems for you."

"Not unless they believe the rumor that you're giving me a better deal on the loan," she joked.

He picked up the nail gun. "That could be a problem."

"For you?"

"For you, after I leave. They might not show their resentment while I'm still around, but after I'm gone…"

Yes. After Jason was gone. What would happen then?

## CHAPTER SEVENTEEN

JASON HAD STASHED his laptop in its bag and was putting on his coat when his cell phone rang. He saw his father's name before he answered.

"Dad?"

"Where are you?" Robert Macland asked without preamble.

"In the bank, about to head home. Something wrong?" His father tended to act like an emperor, inconvenienced by his subjects' unimportant business.

"We're in town."

Jason heard the words before he understood them. "In New York?" he asked, already aware he had that wrong.

"Mother and Father wanted to come back if you were going to be here for Christmas."

"I told you I'd be home for New Year's." His father hadn't seemed to notice Jason never came home for Christmas. None of his siblings put much effort into getting back, either. He felt ridiculous when he realized he was a grown man who'd had too many disappointing Christmases to enjoy them with his family.

"We've rented a house. I'll text you the address."

"How did you find a house on such short notice?"

"Money talks, son. Especially in a tourist town."

Nice.

"You're all here already?"

"Mother and Father and me. Your sisters and brother are planning to come in on Christmas Eve."

Jason couldn't have been more startled. His younger siblings had never lived in Bliss. They knew less than he had about the town.

"A real family celebration." The sarcasm escaped him before he could catch it. His father didn't notice it, however. At least he didn't say anything. Just waited for Jason to speak again. "All right. Send me the address. I'll be over in an hour or so, but Dad?"

"Yeah?"

"We're going to talk about my mother. You

can't duck the questions if we're going to be in the same house."

"I'm ready."

Back at the hotel, Jason changed into jeans and a flannel shirt. He placed calls to his sisters, Beth and Debbie. They didn't answer. His brother, Tom, was just finishing his first semester at college. He didn't answer his phone, either, but texted that he'd call after work.

Much to Robert Macland's chagrin, Tom worked delivering pizzas because he was no more willing than Jason to ask for money from their father.

None of them had mentioned to Jason that they were coming to Bliss for the holidays.

He put the rented house address in his nav and drove to a chalet farther up Bliss Peak than either his or Fleming's house. Smoke drifted out of the three chimneys in the peaked roof. Lights shone in the early evening darkness from most of the oversize windows, which hung on the house like framed photos filled with books and golden shelving and lamps that invited him inside the warm glow.

Jason parked in front of a set of wide steps and got out of the car as half the double front door opened and his grandfather emerged. Dressed in flannel trousers and a crisp white shirt beneath a dark green sweater, Connor Macland looked a decade younger than his seventy-something years.

"How's it going, son?" he asked.

Jason ignored his outstretched hand and hugged his grandfather. "I'm fine. What are you all doing here? Did Dad drag you down so he could check on my work?"

Connor laughed. "More like we dragged him so we could check on you, once Evelynn realized you weren't joining us for the holidays. As per usual."

Nodding, Jason followed his grandfather inside. His small, elegant grandmother was hurrying down the hall, drying her hands on a dish towel.

"Jason, honey," she said, and her accent, still East Tennessee, made him feel as if he really had come home. "You're a little early for dinner, but we'll have a coffee and talk. Are you surprised to see us? I was a little worried we'd be impinging on your work schedule."

"I'm surprised, but happy to set work aside," he said, and he was. They weren't crowding him by bringing the holidays to him. They were welcome in this place that would probably haunt him the rest of his life, with its beauty and its kind people and its gossip and sense of community.

A man could have a family here, of people related to him and people he just cared for. If he were the kind of man who trusted those kinds of people.

"I'm so glad to be back." Evelynn hugged him tight and pulled his face down to hers to kiss his cheek. "Your father always acted as if we'd be betraying him if we came back here. To be honest, your grandfather and I visited on the sly, when your father thought we were elsewhere, but we stood by his edict that we not bring you children."

"Why?" Jason shut the front door and took off his coat in the echoing hall. Their voices bounced off cedar walls and glass skylights. "Why did you let him be such a tyrant?"

"We wanted to make sure you children had a good chance in life," Evelynn said. "To do that we had to make sure he didn't cut us off."

"Like he did your mother," Connor said. "He couldn't use money against us, but we loved you children enough to do whatever he asked."

"You're aware I can hear you?" Robert Macland came out of a room on the landing above the entrance hall. He simply laughed at his detractors. "I've always done what's best for my family. You all know that. Jason, feel up to some skiing before dinner?"

"I didn't bring my things, Dad. Maybe tomorrow?"

"They've had to make snow, but it should be sufficient. I thought I'd visit the office with you tomorrow, if that's satisfactory?"

This one time, his father was signing his paycheck. "Sure, Dad. But I need to speak to you for a second."

Robert waited, not answering. His expression remained bland. Jason began to climb the stairs. "Gran, Grandpa, we'll be out in a minute."

At the top of the stairs, he followed his father into an office. "Now you explain, Dad."

Robert sat behind a desk just made for a man like him. It felt like a Fortune 500 office. He settled into the chair that seated him as if he were on a throne.

Jason sat in the chair across from him, declining to be intimidated. "Now," he said. "My mother says she tried to stay in touch. You say she didn't."

"I kept her letters from you."

Blood rushed to Jason's head. "Why did you do that? Why haven't you ever told me?"

"She gave up," Robert said. "I never would have given up on you. I haven't. I still believe one day you'll come to work for me. And I know you'll forgive me for protecting you from that woman."

"She's a wreck, Dad. I don't know when your friend left her—"

"Or she left him."

"No. She said he cheated on her, and she's alone. I don't think she's had anyone to love in a long time. Including me. I'm not a child. I should have had the opportunity to know her and make my own decisions. You destroyed her like you destroyed our house."

"My house. I bought it. I kept it."

"You let it fall to pieces."

"Because of her." Robert Macland tapped the side of his cheek with his finger, as if he were thinking. "I have no regrets. I couldn't trust her with you, and she doesn't deserve your trust, either."

His self-satisfied tone convinced Jason the argument was pointless. His father would never change. He was always going to be right. Those who did as he asked were accepted. Everyone who made a decision contrary to Robert Macland's would face trouble.

"What else are you hiding from me?" Jason asked.

"You have all my secrets," Robert said, with an amused smirk that annoyed Jason.

"Dad, I'd advise you not to do this again. If I were like you, I'd cut you out of my life right now. As it is, I don't want to be around you."

"But you have no choice because you love my parents unconditionally."

"What do you even know about unconditional love?"

"That there's no place for it in my life," Robert said. "And that's what I've tried to teach you. So you won't let your guard down. You'll thank me someday."

When he'd had three wives who'd prefer to be anywhere but with him? Jason would avoid that fate at all costs.

"I'm getting out of here." He paused. "Do you still have my mother's letters? I'd like to see her side of the last twenty years."

"I trashed them, and before you feel too bad for her, remember that she made choices. I didn't make them for her."

"Right, Dad. None of this is your fault." This was why he'd avoided working for his father in the past. The bitter arrogance was like looking in a mirror of what could be.

Robert followed him out of the office. Jason's grandmother was waiting downstairs, hovering as if she wasn't sure what might have been happening above. She'd prepared herself for the worst.

"Still going out, son?" she asked. "You don't mind skiing in the dark?"

"They light the trails. See you all later."

"Don't break your neck," Evelynn said. Though she smiled, she looked after her middle-aged child with a hint of worry.

"He'll be fine." Her husband tugged her close within the circle of his arms. "Luckiest son of a gun ever born, honey."

"I know. I'm being foolish, but I always worry his luck will run out before he realizes he doesn't rule this world." She pulled away. "Jason, come see what I'm making for dinner. Your sisters should be here within the hour. I'm making their favorite fish and roasting vegetables. They're supposed to text me when it's safe to fire everything."

"Gran, I'm so glad to see you." Her chattering was the loving background music of all the good days in Jason's life. He dumped his coat on a chair by the stairs and followed her to the kitchen. "Coming, Grandpa?"

"I'm going for a walk."

Jason looked back at his grandfather, but Evelynn took his arm. "Not to worry. He gets fed up with your father's egotism, but a walk will cool him down. He's suffered more than any of us for leaving this place. Except maybe you."

"Me?"

"Your mother came back? Is that what I understand?"

"About five years ago."

The kitchen opened onto a view of the mountain, stretching away in a spiky field of evergreen trees that looked slightly gray with fallen snow. A stream foamed white all the way down the incline. Several other chalets clung to the mountain to the east and west, but he couldn't see them without leaning against the glass.

Jason studied the view from the window.

Far above the town of Bliss, they seemed to be all but alone in a winter landscape.

"Does she appear to be all right?" Evelynn asked.

"Not really. She seems to believe the things Dad says about her. She initially said she wanted the house, but I think she just wanted to see it. I didn't remember it. I didn't even know about it."

"No, you wouldn't remember. We left when you were too young, but imagine your life if you'd lived it in the freedom of these mountains rather than within the constrictions of city life, with your father climbing the next rung of every success ladder he could find."

"Success ladder, Gran?"

"You know what I mean." She set a cutting board on the work surface, which was the size of a cafeteria lunch counter.

"I still don't understand why you never brought us here." Meaning him, his sisters and his brother.

She took vegetables from the fridge, which closed with a snick as if it were sucking air from the room and compressing it inside.

"I don't think your father minded so much about Beth and Debbie and Tom, but he wouldn't have wanted you to come. He didn't want your mother to find a way to see you. He didn't want that to happen."

"I didn't even know she wanted to," he said. "Dad told me she never made the slightest effort. I never heard from her, and I don't understand why she'd give up when I was finally old enough that Dad couldn't interfere anymore."

"Your father admitted all this?" Evelynn opened a bag of cauliflower. "He's my son, but I don't understand him. We didn't raise him to be so afraid of loving," she said with a thoughtful, inward look.

"My mother told me, and I asked him. He said she just gave up. She thought I didn't want to hear from her, so I assume that he played us both."

"Honey, Teresa was not a nice lady. She had some habits not suited to taking care of a child." His grandmother spoke in hushed tones, as if the information she had was too shocking to share.

"What do you mean?"

"She used to just run off. With men."

"Run off?"

"Leave for days at a time. She made no

effort to hide her behavior. It was as if she wanted your father to know."

Considering his own rather wasted freshman year of college, during which he'd done anything he thought might shock his disapproving father, Jason wasn't surprised. It had taken him years to understand why he'd acted the way he had, but he knew now. "She was probably trying to get his attention."

"She got it, all right. I felt sorry for her at first. She was such a pretty young thing, and she adored your father when they married, but I believe they soon came to realize what they could expect from each other." Evelynn seemed regretful as she began to clean the ends off the cauliflower. "And by the time they divorced, I didn't even trust her enough to agree that she should see you. The courts gave your father custody without a fight."

"You mean she didn't fight."

Evelynn shook her head. "I don't believe she was in the country. She'd gone to Spain, or Portugal. I can't remember."

"I remember when she left, but I also saw her a few days ago. She's remorseful, Gran. I don't think it's just an act."

"Maybe not. Maybe she realizes what she truly lost by leaving your father."

"She lost everything. Literally."

"I mean you. You forget, the doorman called me down to you on the street that day." Evelynn set down the knife as if she were going to hug him again, but her cell phone rang. She picked it up and answered. "Debbie, are you and your sister on the ground? How long until you get here?"

Smiling in anticipation of seeing his sisters, Jason went in search of his grandfather. He didn't need to talk about his parents any longer. They'd both made horrible choices, but he'd tried to work at some sort of relationship with his father. The more time he spent with him, the less reasonable Jason's own attitude toward his mother seemed.

Or maybe Fleming's soft heart had begun to tenderize him.

"Gran," he called over his shoulder. "I'm going to find Grandpa and ask him if he wants to go out for a while. We'll be back."

FLEMING WAS UNDER a Christmas tree, replacing the skirt because someone had bought the original ivory-and-gold one she'd set up. The shop door's sleigh bells jingled at her back.

"Hello," she called. "Happy holidays. I'll be right with you. Feel free to look around."

"We'll do that," Jason's voice said.

She straightened so abruptly she almost turned the tree over. The ornaments jangled, sounding like bells around her head. Something must have fallen off the other side, because there was the unmistakable sound of breaking glass as it hit the floor.

"Careful," Jason said.

She backed out and scrambled to her feet. "What are you doing—" She stopped. A tall, older man stood at Jason's side. Their resemblance was unmistakable. "This must be your father."

"My grandfather," Jason said. He smiled at the other man. "Grandpa, this is Fleming Harris. She owns this shop. Fleming, this is my grandfather, Connor Macland."

"Fleming," He shook her hand in greeting. "I remember your mother, Katherine. She was just a young thing when she worked over at the diner for a while. I'd heard she opened this place. How's she doing?"

"She's fine. She and her husband, Hugh,

live in Knoxville. He's a cardiologist," Fleming said, rattling on as usual when she felt awkward. "They're coming home in a few days."

"I hope we'll get a chance to see Katherine again. My grandson and I have come to stock up for our own holiday celebration."

"You're staying at the Benjamins' place, too? I'm glad Lyle could find room for you." Maybe Jason had known his grandfather was coming. She looked at him, but he was giving nothing away.

"We've rented a house on the mountain," Mr. Macland said. "Which brings me to the reason we've stopped by. Jason and I are picking up a Christmas tree, and we need decorations. My grandson thought you could help us out."

"I'd be glad to," she said, rubbing her head where she'd run into something hard in the tree. "We have quite a variety. Do you want a theme?"

So many people preferred themes of color or types of ornaments these days. Like Jason, she preferred just pulling the ornaments out of their boxes and putting them on the tree as they appeared.

"I think we'll look around, choose what we like."

"Can I offer you coffee? Water?"

"No." Mr. Macland scanned the ornaments hanging from branches, and the others stacked on shelves. "We need to get this done. The other children will be home soon, and we want to have everything ready."

Fleming looked at Jason. The other children? His brother and sisters? He shrugged and joined his grandfather.

Fleming checked with the other customers in the store and then went to the counter, biting her tongue to keep from interrogating both Macland men. Jason had brought his whole family home for Christmas? Or had they shown up because he was here?

During the next hour, he and his grandfather mingled with the other customers, slowly collecting a wide selection of ornaments they brought to the counter. After they finished foraging, there was a pile that would have made Santa proud—if Santa made ornaments to put on trees, rather than toys to put beneath them.

Such a large sale made her a little light-headed. If only every visitor in town needed to stock up like this.

The two men argued a little over making the payment. Jason said the whole thing was down to his father. Mr. Macland pointed out that Jason's father happened to be his son.

Fleming didn't understand, but she was happy to take their money.

"You're doing all right tonight," Jason said.

"Better since you all came in." She grinned, basking in her good fortune.

"You have an amazing selection," Mr. Macland said, and somehow he lost the fight to present his credit card.

She charged the purchase to Jason's. "My mother built up the business all through my childhood," she said.

"I'd love to see your mother again. Maybe we can all get together for dinner before Christmas Eve."

"Maybe we could meet…" she glanced at Jason "…after caroling practice, unless you're going to quit now that your family's arrived."

His grandfather looked at him as if she'd suggested he fly the tree home.

"I'm not quitting," Jason said.

"When did you join the carolers? How long are you planning to stay here, Jason?"

"Until I finish the bank's business," he said. "Caroling isn't a lifetime commitment."

Fleming looked up, meeting his gaze, not bothering to hide that his quick denial hurt her. He had other places to be. He didn't need a family or friends. They got in the way of his business.

But what if she asked him if it could be different? What if Jason, letting love into his life instead of fending it off, was a Christmas miracle?

# CHAPTER EIGHTEEN

FLEMING STUMBLED INTO the kitchen on the Monday of Christmas week to find her mother stirring hot cocoa at the stove. Katherine turned, her smile slightly anxious. The smile of a mother who thought her daughter's heart was broken.

"Mom, what are you doing here? Is Hugh with you?" She glanced at the clock over the kitchen sink. It was barely past 7:00 a.m. "I didn't hear you all come in."

"The house was so quiet we thought you must be asleep. We were exhausted so we just climbed into bed. Hugh's still upstairs." She began to stir again as Fleming hugged her. "I heard from some friends that Jason Macland's family arrived in town."

"I met his grandfather. They came in and bought ornaments for a tree. They're staying for Christmas in a chalet farther up the mountain."

Katherine still didn't look up. "Is that all you know?"

"Meaning what?" Fleming took cups out of the cabinet. "What did you hear that made you rush home several days early?"

"That maybe Jason's family thought you weren't good enough for the chosen son, so they staged an intervention with the goal of dragging him back to New York."

Fleming couldn't believe what she was hearing, but she laughed. "I'd love to think of myself as an addiction, but your sources have the situation totally wrong."

"How wrong?"

"What are you talking about, Mom? His grandparents wanted to see their town again. His dad came with them, and Jason's sisters and brother came, too. For Christmas. Not because I'm some femme fatale the firstborn can't resist. It's ridiculous."

Katherine sagged against the front of the stove. "I'm relieved to hear that, but I don't think I'm wrong about your feelings for him. You do care. I give you credit for trying not to, and maybe you're the last to know, but you are in love with that man."

Fleming wondered if she should pinch herself. "Is this a nightmare?"

"It could be, but thankfully I hear he's not like his father. Robert wanted to settle down with every pretty woman he had feelings for. Three wives later, the women are wising up, not him. But his son doesn't stay in one place long enough to let himself think of getting serious in a relationship."

It wasn't as funny now. Those were Fleming's own thoughts. Her worst fears.

"I don't want to discuss this. I don't know how I feel about Jason. How can I explain it to you?"

"Because you need to face facts and decide how much you want to be with him before he leaves and your chance for happiness goes with him."

"Mother—"

"I won't say more. I was so incensed at the idea that those people might have come here with the idea of insulting you that Hugh and I rushed to defend you. But I realize that you have to sort this out on your own. If you love Jason, you should ask him to stay. So that you can give each other a chance."

"I feel sick." Because her mother's words

rang true. With every passing day Fleming had been more aware of her growing sense of dread. She dreaded the day Jason turned his back on her for the last time.

"Do you think you'll see him tonight?" her mother asked.

Fleming pushed her hands through her hair. "I don't know." The caroling. "If he comes out to sing."

"Have you told him how you feel? Have you asked him to stay?"

"I haven't made a great effort to hide that I'd like him to stay in Bliss, but how can I ask that, Mom? He wouldn't be happy here. The town is too small for him, but it's the perfect size for me, and I don't want to live anywhere else."

"Think about that," Katherine said. "Not that I regret keeping our home here, or letting you stay in your school and remain in the hometown you loved, but think of the lost years I took from Hugh and me."

"I still don't see why you didn't go live with Hugh. At the time I accepted it, but now I question why we didn't just move to Knoxville to live with him as a family."

Katherine began to pour hot chocolate into

the cups Fleming had set on the counter. "You know how it was with your father?"

"I know how I imagine it was, and that's bad enough."

"I loved him, Fleming. With all my heart. I wanted our life to be good. I wanted to make him happy, and I never knew how. I lost him. So when Hugh loved me, I couldn't help being afraid I would do something that would make him leave." She licked her lips, apparently made dry by the truth. "I was so afraid of losing my relationship with Hugh that I found excuses to avoid committing to him. I can tell you, I went to him in the nick of time. My husband-to-be back then was patient, but he wanted the kind of love he'd given me so freely. He deserved that kind of love."

Fleming could barely see her mother through a haze of tears. She tried to stand, but she wasn't sure her legs would support her. "Mom, am I so wrong? I know Jason cares about me, but he's never said anything to lead me on. I don't think he loves me."

"I don't think he trusts love. He's never seen it except from his grandparents."

"But shouldn't they be enough? They've

been together for decades. Why isn't their example the one he believes in?"

"Ask him."

"I don't know how."

"With words."

Before Fleming could argue again, the front door blew open and Hugh came in, shivering in his robe and pajamas, brandishing a plastic-covered newspaper.

"I found this down at the end of the driveway," he said. "In a snowbank. If we'd slept in, we never would have found it. Have you given the paper carrier his Christmas gift yet?"

Fleming composed herself while Hugh came down the hall. "Mom thought you were still in bed."

"No. Hungry for news and breakfast. Breakfast I was sure of. The paper I barely found in time."

"Well, I'm not going to stiff the paper guy at the holidays because he has a bad throwing arm."

"Sorry." Hugh kissed Fleming's forehead and then turned toward her mother. "I must be cranky, half frozen and hungry. How's breakfast coming along, Katherine?"

"I'm putting the cinnamon rolls in the oven right now. Will that be all right with you, Fleming?"

"If they're done by the time I have to leave for work." She headed down the hall toward the stairs.

"I'm going with you today."

Fleming froze, one foot on the first step. "Mom?"

Oven sounds answered her, the door opening and closing. Hugh made a production of sniffing as he joined her mother. "I can't wait until those are done. Are you making that cream cheese frosting?"

"It's already in the fridge."

"Mom," Fleming said again.

Her mother came to the kitchen doorway. "What's up?"

"Why are you coming to work with me today? What do you think I'm doing wrong?"

"What?"

Fleming tugged at her hair, trying to smooth the waves that always did just what they wanted, anyway. She was a grown woman. "It's my responsibility from now on. If you want to come visit, you're more than welcome, but if you're only coming because you don't think I know what I'm doing…"

"What do you mean?" Katherine put her hand on the doorjamb. "I've never treated you like that."

Fleming sighed with remorse and ran her moist palms down her pajama legs. "I'm sorry. I just feel responsible, and I don't want you to feel obligated to jump in and rescue me."

"I want to spend the day with my daughter, in the shop where we used to spend our days." Grinning, her mom turned from the doorway. "I need that cocoa now, Hugh. See if Fleming has marshmallows."

"Better yet, want me to add some brandy?"

"Tempting, but if I'm going in to the shop with her, homemade cocoa will be restorative enough."

Her mother's hot chocolate was positively gourmet. If they ever had to sell the shop, they could make a fortune with her recipe. How many people had stopped in for it each holiday and then bought something while they drank?

"I made snickerdoodles last night," Fleming called. "If you put some in bags we could take them along."

"Perfect," Katherine agreed. "Hurry now. Breakfast will be ready by the time you're dressed."

"I'm on my way."

Walking into the store a few hours later was strange, with her mother at her side again, but it also felt like Christmas. Soon they were busy with folks buying their last-minute gifts, a first ornament for a new baby, a special ornament for a child in a family where the parents collected them as Fleming's mom had.

They were also apparently one of the last places in town that still had strings of lights. Fleming had thought she'd be sending them back to the supplier in January, but they all but walked out the door on their own.

"Who could have guessed?" Katherine asked after they sold the sixth set.

"Two to go," Fleming said. "By Christmas they'll be gone."

"Only three days. We just have to sell one per day." Katherine glanced out the window. "Speaking of which, how much longer do you think he'll be in town?"

Fleming turned. Jason, bundled in his wool overcoat, was hurrying past the shop He turned his head for a brief nod. Fleming ignored the way her breathing seemed to catch. Every day she expected him to be gone. "Wonder if they'll all go back to New York together after Christmas?"

"Do you have a gift for him?"

"I bought him action figures."

"Action what?"

"I ordered them. They were on a cartoon television show he used to watch. I could only afford the hero and heroine, and a cat the hero rode that was apparently also his best friend."

"A cat he rode. I don't remember this. And why would a grown man want them?"

"He's got one from the set—it was something he always wanted. I found the others."

"That's thoughtful. They can't have been inexpensive. How do you plan to get them to him? Are you meeting to exchange gifts?"

Fleming attempted a silencing glance. "I thought I could ask Lyle Benjamin to put them in his hotel room, but now I don't know if he's staying over at the chalet with the rest of his family. I haven't seen him in a few days."

"Maybe you can take them to the chalet. You could give them to him in person."

The possibility shook her. "Not in front of his family. He might think I'm a snoop—intruding." She decided to flee this conversation. "I'm going over to the coffee shop. Want me to bring you anything?"

"We're running out of milk in the back. Why don't you pick up a gallon?"

On the way to the little convenience store that huddled between a church and a trendy boutique, Fleming stopped at a shop called Remembrance of Things Past. She spied a train running in the window, through their version of the obligatory Bliss-based shop's miniature snowy village. She couldn't help remembering Jason admiring the trains in her store.

Maybe a train was a better idea. Something he could give his own family one day.

She eased inside, not wanting to draw attention to herself with the small, tinkling bell that announced visitors.

She walked straight to a shelf of vintage trains. She really thought Jason might enjoy one of his own. Next Christmas, he could set it up and remember his time in Bliss.

Even if he set it up under a tree he shared with some other woman? A woman he loved enough to stay for? And later, the children they had together?

Fleming's heart broke a little at the thought.

But it wasn't her business. She had too much imagination. Good for writing. Not so great for living.

Nevertheless, she wandered the cluttered aisles of the little store. It wasn't as elegantly laid out as most of the antiques shops in town, but it was filled with treasures. In the past she'd found yo-yos and vintage games and nutcrackers that she'd used to decorate Mainly Merry Christmas.

In the fourth aisle she perused, she found another train, this one in a ragged box. It had been made before she was born, and it only had three of the four cars that were pictured on the lid, but it was just what she'd imagined for Jason.

Maybe it would be what he'd love.

"Adding to your collection?" a voice asked at her side.

Sam Leslie, the proprietor, had walked up so silently she hadn't heard him. "Hi," she said. "Does it work?"

"Sure does." He took the box and tilted the lid to peer inside. "Anyway, it did last time I set it up. Want to me to do it again for you?"

"No. If you think it works, that's good enough for me. I'll take it home and try it out."

"Okay." He settled the lid again. "If it doesn't work, bring it back."

"Thanks, Sam."

They agreed on a price, and Sam wrapped the box in Santa-covered tissue and then tucked it into a deep shopping bag. Fleming hoped her mother would be busy when she returned. She carried the bag with its handles over her arm as she lugged a gallon of milk back to the store.

She managed to stash the train beneath the front counter before her mother came out of the rear.

"You remembered the milk," Katherine said. Then she stopped, looking around. "But where's your coffee?"

"I forgot. I'll just have another hot chocolate after you make it."

"Good for the waistline." Katherine hugged her. "I worry you haven't been eating enough. You look as if you're losing weight." She started back toward the kitchen area. "You took a long time picking up the milk."

"I walked a little first," Fleming said, uncomfortable with lying, but more reluctant to admit she'd been buying Jason something else that might have more meaning.

"You needed a little break from my advice?"

"Not at all." Fleming followed her and hugged her from behind, maneuvering around the now-open milk container in her mother's hand. "I'm so glad you and Hugh came home."

Katherine's smile warmed Fleming from the inside. "Thanks, honey. Hugh says I should give you more space, and he keeps reminding me my name isn't on the deed anymore. He thought you might be afraid I didn't trust you with the details of running the store."

"It's not that. I came so close to failure, I don't want you to worry that I'm inept and I'm going to throw away this place that means so much to *both* of us."

"I would love it if I could come back and work for you someday, after Hugh retires and we move here."

"You really think he's willing to do that?"

"We both plan on it. The condo is comfortable and handy, but I miss these mountains just as you would, and Hugh feels as if this could be his home, too."

"Then I'd love for you to come home to Mainly Merry Christmas when Hugh's ready."

"Good. And we'll both remember that I'll be working for you this time around. I'm glad that's settled." Katherine looked back from pouring milk into a huge saucepan on the stove. "Do you mind if I ask what you think of the next few months?"

Fleming would welcome her advice. "I worry about January's takings, but I'll do my best to hang on and take stock of my position in, say, April, and then again in July. I don't want to lose everything if I do end up in trouble again. I'd probably try to sell before that happened."

Her mother's smile signaled approval. "I'm glad to hear you take a pragmatic approach. That sounds like a plan."

"I might talk it over with Jason. He's offered to help me with changes to make the business more profitable."

"I'd take him up on it. His father wasn't like him, you know. He would have foreclosed on all the loans Mr. Paige gave out. He wouldn't have given a second thought to the families that kind of loss would affect."

"He might have if the town's economy was in danger."

"You should ask Jason about that." Katherine huffed. "I'm surprised Robert sent his son back here. If you'd asked me what I thought he might do, I'd have said he would have foreclosed on everyone and then closed the bank."

Fleming passed her mother the box of rich, dark chocolate she used to make her cocoa. "That sounds suspiciously like the man Jason describes."

"He describes his father to you?"

"Do you know they owned a house here? No one else has ever lived in it since they left. Robert just walked away and changed the locks so that Jason's mother could never get back inside."

Katherine broke up chunks of chocolate and eased them thoughtfully into the double boiler. "I heard she left him for his best friend after they went to New York."

"She did," Fleming said, realizing too late

that she was revealing how close she and Jason had become through talking about their families. Her mother didn't seem to notice.

"I forgot about the house, and I was so busy I guess I never noticed none of them came back. The Maclands all moved to New York at one time. We thought they just felt too big for Bliss with their success." She stirred the chocolate with a silicon spoon. "Not that the town grows as quickly as they did. You can understand they'd want something bigger."

"I guess." Fleming had wanted something bigger herself until she'd gone to school in Washington, DC. After she'd graduated, she couldn't get back fast enough to her beloved mountains with their smoky mists and steamy, verdant green summers.

The bell over their door rang as someone new came in. Katherine glanced that way. "We should get back to work."

"Yes." Fleming went into the store, glancing at the shelf beneath the counter where her train waited. She couldn't help hoping her mother wouldn't notice her new gift for Jason.

It was a train meant for building a family tradition. Maybe if she gave it to him he'd understand she was giving him a piece of what their future Christmases could be. If they could be together.

Or she could guard her heart and leave that train right where it was, rather than risk the most painful rejection ever.

## CHAPTER NINETEEN

THE NEXT DAY, Katherine and Hugh went out in the car to wander the mountains. Fleming managed to hide her relief at having some privacy. Jason hadn't shown up for caroling the night before. She wasn't sure if she was relieved or disappointed that they hadn't been able to talk. She wrapped the train for him and waited for courage to arrive.

People were in and out of the store, but tomorrow was Christmas Eve, and the ornament and Christmas gewgaw business appeared to have leveled off. Late in the evening, Fleming saw Jason stroll by, talking on his phone. He nodded her way with a smile that literally took her breath away, but when she smiled back, he stopped in his tracks.

His gaze seemed like a mirror of hers, warm, reluctant, resolute. Longing.

She wasn't wrong. He kept his eyes on her

for as long as he could, until he'd passed the window.

Fleming gave him a few minutes. If she didn't go to him now, she might never be able to. Tomorrow, he'd be with his family. For all she knew, he might already have cleared his desk to leave right after the new year. That had been his original plan.

Breathing hard, trembling as she felt her pulse banging like a gong inside her body, she picked up the train and started toward the door of the store. Reflected in the glass, the package looked big and festive. She was about to take Jason a Christmas gift in his hotel room, and anyone—everyone—could see her intentions.

If she waited to find a shopping bag, she might lose her nerve. She locked the store and marched through the snow. Once upon a time her mother would have cautioned her that a lady didn't chase a man down and ask him to love her.

But a lady might have to if she was afraid he'd leave town and never come back.

Jason was rebuilding his house here—shouldn't she wait for him to come to her?

No, she had to know.

At the hotel, the reception desk was empty. She sped up the stairs, holding her box in front of her like a shield.

She knocked on Jason's door and barely managed to stand still. He opened it, already having shed his jacket and tie.

"Fleming." He looked down at the box. "What have you done?"

She swallowed. "I have a gift for you." She held it out. "And a question."

He opened the door wider. "Come on in. I have something for you, too." He went to his desk and got a small, rectangular box.

"Thank you," she said, her insides too twisted to manage more. "I had a speech."

"Why did you need one?" He closed the door behind her. "Can I take that? It looks heavy."

No. She gripped it in front of her, thinking she should have let Christmas Eve come and go, to see if Jason changed his mind on his own about leaving her behind. That would have been right.

Not this. Not begging for his attention.

She handed him the gift. "I thought it would be perfect for you."

"Should I open it? No, not until you open yours."

"I need to talk to you first."

He came closer, setting the box down. "What's wrong? Has something happened at the shop? Are you all right?" He ran the backs of his fingers over her cheek. "Tell me, Fleming."

"I..." The words wouldn't come. She'd tried to tell herself for so long that she couldn't be with him. Now, the time had come when he'd spoken of leaving, and she couldn't accept it. "I care about you," she said, her voice breaking. "I don't want you to leave. Or at least not to stay gone forever. I brought you this because I wondered if you could think of caring for me. If you could consider what life might be like in Bliss, if we cared for each other."

He froze. "Fleming." He stepped back, opening the box, but not really seeing it. "I do care about you," he said. "I haven't wanted to, because your life is here and mine is not. I might not be enough for you."

She didn't understand. He'd thought about her in the same way? "You are enough."

"I work long hours, in a lot of different places," he said. "I don't want to repeat my parents' mistake. My father's business demanded his time, and my mother got fed up with it. She felt so neglected and isolated that she left. How could I risk letting that happen to you?"

"Nothing happens that we don't choose," Fleming said. "I've been afraid, too. I love every inch of Bliss, every voice I hear, every leaf on every tree, I've been safe here. In fact, I'm terrified I'm not sophisticated enough, well-traveled enough, or interesting enough for you. But we meet on a level of understanding I never expected to have with any man, and I don't want to lose that. I don't want to lose you."

"Fleming, I've had relationships in the past. I've believed they would last, but I never committed. It's not in me. I want us to be together, but I can't promise you forever."

He touched her again, his hand smoothing her hair back from her face. He lowered his head and kissed her forehead. Tenderly, he took her mouth and kissed her in a way that felt like a contradiction of everything he'd just said.

But she knew he was offering only right

now. This minute, maybe the next, or even a few months.

It wasn't enough for her.

"No." She pulled away from him. "I had to ask," she said, her heart breaking. Shame washed over her as she thought about everything she'd said. She'd bared her soul to a man who didn't care for souls. "But I think I misunderstood who you are—not that you ever lied to me. I'm not blaming you."

Jason stared at her. His hands flexed. "I've thought of this," he said. "I've wanted to tell you how happy you make me every time you laugh. How you made me believe in Christmas again. How your joy becomes my joy when you're singing or playing with the children in your shop or even just trying to think of a way to sell one more glass Santa. But nothing lasts, Fleming. You and I would not last. Your life is here. I'd feel buried alive here."

"Your grandparents have lasted," she said, "and they threw everything aside so you'd have an example of love to believe in."

"Real life made a bigger impression on me than the million-to-one shot that two people could find love without eventually destroying each other." His regret was a sadness that enveloped her. "My grandparents are the exception."

He sounded as certain as he had about the facts and figures that meant she'd been on the verge of losing Mainly Merry Christmas.

She'd thought that had been her worst fear. Now she knew the truth. She'd fallen in love with Jason Macland, sometime between making ornaments and building steps and talking about the experiences that had honed them into the closed off, lonely people who'd met in his office.

She would love Jason all her life, and she wasn't enough for him.

"Goodbye," she said, and walked out of his room. Out of his life.

Love was all or nothing for her.


"What are you doing up here today?"

Jason turned from staring at the train, still in its open box, in the middle of the living room in his abandoned house.

Teresa stood in the doorway. She looked worried about him.

"I could ask you the same thing," he answered.

"I was thinking about the Christmases you and your father and I shared while we still loved each other." She came into the room, sliding her hand over the wall. "You've been working. I noticed the new stairs out front, and there's primer on this plaster."

"I had this crazy idea that I could renovate the house," he said. "This room had the least damage, so I cleaned the walls and started priming." He'd been avoiding Fleming, even before her visit to his hotel room. He'd already known he was in too deep.

He hadn't known her mom and stepfather were in town, and that she'd been missing carol practice, too, until someone asked him why they'd both quit.

"You've started making the house beautiful again." Teresa eased closer, as if she were afraid of his possible reaction. "What's with the train?"

"It was a gift," he said. The card lay on top of the cars, the words Fleming had written taunting him.

"It's cute. Does it run?"

"I think so. It seems to need a tree."

"I love that tradition," his mother said. "We used to have one under the tree when you were a baby. It fascinated you." She frowned. "Did your father give it to you? I hear he's in town."

Jason had been avoiding him, too, as well as the rest of the family. He felt like a fraud. "Fleming gave it to me. The woman who owns the Christmas shop."

"I thought you were interested in her. The way you looked at each other made me think—"

"Do you need something? Is that why you're here?" He cut her off midsentence. He and Teresa had enough problems of their own. There was no need to bring Fleming into it.

"Jason, are you all right?"

He looked at her for a moment. She sat down and started taking pieces of the train out of the box.

"No, I'm not all right," he said. He'd hurt the woman he loved. Even if it was for her own good, he hated himself for the pain he'd caused Fleming.

"Because of Fleming?"

"Yes. And our family, and the way I am."

His mother began to piece the train track together. There was plenty of it. "Help me," she said. "Come down here, and tell me about the way you are."

"You're not my mother now."

"I am," she said, "whether you like it or not. I don't think either of us knows how to start over, but maybe we can begin by being friends. Friends listen. You help me with this track and I'll listen to you."

He didn't talk at first. They simply set up the track in a circle that spread around half the room.

"So what are you like, Jason?"

He thought for a moment. "I'm honest."

"And you hurt that girl? She wanted you, but you don't want her?"

"I love her," he said. "Right now, I can't think of anything except how much I love her. I don't want to spend another day without her. She makes me feel as if life is good and right."

Teresa lifted her gaze, her eyes not as bright a blue as he remembered. "That sounds horrible. I can see why you're upset."

"It won't last. Fleming has been sheltered in these mountains all her life, and she believes in fairy tales. I live in a different world, and I know how it works."

"You have expertise in the ways people can hurt each other." His mom crawled over the track, back to the box, and took out the first train car. "You could choose not to hurt her."

"You and Dad planned to lie and cheat and divorce?"

"And make you believe you weren't lovable? Neither of us—not even your father—planned that. He was obviously trying to protect you even if hurting me was the bonus he got. He didn't trust me with you because I wanted a man's love more. At least I thought I did, until it was too late to make things right."

"I'm glad you told me that, and I wish I'd waited to hear it when we spoke before, but it doesn't fix anything."

She set the locomotive on the track and hooked up the other two cars. Then she folded her hands with a frown. "What was I thinking? We have no power."

"We can't will that train to run, and I can't will life to be what I want," he said. "I can't pretend I believe in forever."

His mother came back to him. She sat in front of him, crossing her legs. "I had about five good years. No, three. Three amazing, happy, beautiful, unbelievable good years that were like every fairy tale you refuse to believe."

"And then they ended," he said. "I remember how they ended. For all of us."

"Because your father didn't pay attention, and I was not kind. I didn't know how to ask for what I wanted. I demanded, because I thought I had the right, just like I did with you in that letter. I get mean when I'm angry."

"I don't respond to mean."

"I know, and I hate to be ignored. I was afraid you'd send me away me, just the way your father did."

"Mom, you couldn't expect him to welcome you fresh from his best friend's arms." He'd called her Mom. She didn't seem to notice, and he decided to accept it. She was his mother.

"I was wrong about so much," she said, "but I felt I had the right to expect my husband would put me before his business. He thought he was giving me his success. He should have asked me if that was the happiness I wanted. We made unspeakable mistakes, and we lost our forever."

"I won't do that," Jason said. "I won't see a child of mine watch me drive away to a new life. Fleming expects the promise of a future without that ending."

He reached for the card and handed it to his mother. She read the words, Fleming's hope for a happily ever after. She read it again, and her eyes were moist when she looked up.

"It could be that simple."

He shook his head.

"I wish it could," he said. "But I care about her too much to pretend I trust myself. No one stays."

"But what if you work on today and just let the future show up?" Teresa balanced the card on top of the locomotive. "If your father had come home on time for dinner three nights of the week and paid attention to me for an hour, I could have tried to understand. I didn't require much. Just a little laughter. Some affection that reminded me I was special to him. If I had understood then that he was showing me his love with every new win he had at the office, maybe we'd still be working on our forever. Every day. One day at a time."

"You know it's not that easy."

"I remember a night when we shared a sandwich after I set the kitchen on fire, cooking dinner. I literally set the place ablaze. And while we ate the sandwich, your father said he could build more kitchens, but there was only one me." She laughed through tears. "That was happiness. That would have kept me from looking at any other man."

"You looked because that's who you are," he said. "Like Dad is. But I won't be that person."

"Let me finish. I had three amazing years, and I've had so many more to live with regret and pain I can't describe to you, but I wouldn't trade one minute of those three. I've never known love like that again. I broke it as much as Robert did, and if I could somehow go back, I wouldn't look anywhere but straight into our future."

Jason couldn't imagine his mother's imbalanced scales defined a good life.

"I believe that if you protect those good days by not allowing distractions—anyone or anything—to chip away at the love between the two of you, you can be happy."

He stared at her. Leaps of faith were not his first instinct.

Because of fear? He hated fear. If his mother and father hadn't been afraid of being alone…

Teresa stood. "Maybe I have no right to say these things to you."

"I asked." He smiled. "And I listened."

"Learn something from the mistakes your father and I made."

He'd thought he had learned all those years ago—that he was not lovable. That love wasn't possible. But his mother hadn't mentioned one thing about that. She'd described a marriage two angry, unbending people had destroyed with their own selfish inability to share a life.

And he believed in her regret.

"Goodbye, son. Merry Christmas."

"Goodbye." He walked her to the front door. "Come back if you want. I've hired a contractor, and the house will be repaired. You're welcome to come and see the progress."

She turned with a smile that looked utterly real. "I would love to watch this house come back to life."

She seemed to mean more than he'd meant. Jason watched her drive away and then he returned to the living room.

He picked up the card Fleming had left in the box.

"This could be our train, around our tree, every Christmas morning for all our years."

How hard had that card been for her to write, when the one thing she feared was being left behind?

If she could imagine him staying, maybe he could comprehend making one really good day with the woman he loved, and then another, and some more.

He still didn't let himself count on all the next days they might be lucky enough to have, but he knew he would never be unkind to her, and she didn't know how to be unkind.

He could do a day at a time, if only Fleming would give him a chance. If she could forgive him for not trusting her, not trusting love. This could be the beginning of their future.

If he loved her, why couldn't he give her his best? A better version of himself than he'd ever believed he could be?

FOR THE FIRST time in her adult life, Fleming lurked at home, a Scrooge-like kind of hermit. Her mother tried to persuade her that letting Jason know how he'd hurt her only gave him power over her.

Fleming didn't care. The power was in the love she couldn't smother, like a fire that wouldn't stop burning. The passing of time might help, but for now she didn't trust herself to see him again.

On Christmas Eve, he called. Fleming refused to answer the phone her mother brought her as she and Hugh shared a bowl of popcorn while watching their favorite holiday movie.

It would be all right. Jason would leave town soon, and life would go back to normal. The thought made Fleming want to cry.

Early on Christmas morning, her cell phone woke her, vibrating on her nightstand. She lifted it, but when she saw Jason's name on the screen, she set it back down and silenced it.

She ignored his voice mail message for a few minutes before curiosity got the better of her.

She braced herself for Jason's reasonable tone. No doubt he'd offer some sensible reason they should forget their last conversation had ever happened.

But his voice sounded different, richer, urgent. "I love you," he said without preamble. "I was wrong. Come to the house this morning before everyone else is awake. I love you, Fleming. I can't imagine how to stop loving you."

That last convinced her, though she could barely hear over the rush of her pulse in her ears. Jason would have tried very hard to stop loving her. He'd convinced her of that. If he couldn't, she'd better find out what he had to say.

She dressed quickly and slipped out of the house, leaving a note for her mother and Hugh on the kitchen counter to say she was all right and she'd be back.

In the dark Christmas morning, she drove up the mountain, but she knew the way to Jason's home.

There were lights. New ones, twinkling from the porch roof and the doorways. When Fleming got out of her car, she heard the low growl of a generator.

"Jason?" She ran up the porch steps. They were totally steady now beneath her feet. Still, it was like running through quicksand in a dream, where the harder she ran, the slower she went.

"Jason?" She called him again, and any-one who heard her voice would have known she was desperate. She pounded on the newly hung front door. If he left Bliss without her, he'd be taking the best parts of her with him.

"I'm coming," he called. She heard a clatter from inside. As if someone had dropped an old-fashioned sewing machine down a set of stairs.

She tried the big, heavy glass knob, but the door was locked. "Are you all right? I can't get to you."

"Hold on."

She heard him release the dead bolt and the door swung open. Snowflakes swirled in with her as she entered. She stumbled to a halt as she saw a typewriter that had to be a hundred years old lying on its side in the wide foyer, and Jason leaning over to pick it up.

"What's going on?" she asked.

"Sorry about this. I was almost ready for you."

"We can't wait for you to be ready. I can't wait." Those weren't the right words, but she couldn't find better ones. Blurting "I love you" hadn't been right the other day. "Can you love me?" had been even more wrong.

"I have something for you," he said. "Come upstairs with me."

"I got your message." For some reason, she'd started to cry. She brushed at the tears on her face.

"Don't say anything," he said, "at least not until you see what I have for you."

"You already gave me a gift."

"Which you left behind." He straightened, letting the typewriter thump to the floor. He took her hands and pulled her close, holding her with heart-shattering tenderness. "I want to give you what makes you happy."

"*You* make me happy. Even when you frustrate me and upset me and scare me."

"Scare you? Because of the store, you mean?"

"I'm not talking about the store." She was getting this wrong. She pulled away. "Losing you scares me. You don't want to be attached. You don't see the need for it, but I need you, and I want you to need me. That's everything I dream of. Us, being part of each other."

He stared down at her, his gaze indulgent, his smile a little stunned.

"You're happy?" she asked, because she couldn't quite tell. He'd said he loved her.

"Will you please stop talking and come upstairs with me?"

She gave him her hands again. He turned, pulling her behind him up the wide staircase until they reached the spacious landing.

She stared.

"It's yours," he said. "Your space, where you can make all your dreams come true."

"What did you do?" she asked, sounding harsh when really she felt grateful and happy and best of all, loved.

He'd turned the landing into an office. A small desk and comfortable chair waited for her in front of the round window overlooking the beautiful mountains—the landscape that owned her, body and soul.

Sunlight had faded the secondhand rug that created the boundaries of the little office area, but fat cabbage roses and leaves wound in a woolen circle of welcome. There were small wooden filing cabinets, scratched and bruised and well-loved, that she would always cherish. She couldn't wait to file her printed manuscripts. And even her rejections.

"Look at this." He went to an old-fashioned turntable and moved its needle onto a record. Slowly, the strains of Massenet's "Thaïs" filled the landing and the stairwell, and echoed through the house.

"We'll all hear the music that inspires you," he said. "While you're working we'll be with you."

"We?" She thought she knew what he meant, but she needed to hear him say it. "You were so certain we didn't have a future."

"You told me once that I didn't stay because I hadn't found the place that tied me."

"Or the people."

"The woman," he said, pressing his forehead to hers, warming her skin with his. "You said your life here was a suit of clothes that fit. Well, you are my place. My place will always be with you."

Her breath caught, and she wrapped her arms around him.

"I may have to build my own cell tower on this mountain so I can work from here, but this is our place now, if you'll have it and me."

"And maybe when you travel, I can drag myself out of these mountains I love."

"That I love, too."

She laughed with unadulterated, perfect joy. "I'm still interested in how you define *we*."

"That's you and I. With our sons and daughters. We'll make meals while you write, and we'll wash the dog and change the cat litter..."

"So many chores." She took shelter in the warmth of his body. In her belief in his love. "Shouldn't I help? You and these children and the dogs and the cats can't do everything."

"But you won't be shouldering the whole load," he said, "and you won't be responsible for anyone else's happiness."

"Except that loving each other makes us happy," she said. "What changed your mind?"

"I talked to my mother, believe it or not, and she told me that she wouldn't trade the good times she had with my father even to erase all the bad years. She asked me to consider the future in increments of days instead of all at once." Jason kissed Fleming, his touch loving and sweet and certain, spreading warmth through her whole body. "And I know you. I forgot that I know who you are. I believe in you."

"And I can believe in you?" she asked.

He grimaced in silent acceptance of the pain in her question. "I promise you can believe in me. I won't hurt you.

"But why did you push me away?"

"Maybe I was running, like my dad did,

like my mom did the day she drove away from our apartment in New York. They couldn't make something work, so they moved on to the next thing. They kept moving forward, as if the detritus they left behind didn't matter to anyone. But I won't move without you, Fleming, and you will always matter most to me. I'm sorry I didn't know how to accept the gift of your love, but if you offer it again, I'll make sure you know every day of our lives how precious you are to me."

She was afraid, but he was different. She felt the change in him in the hoarse strength of his voice. "If you were to give up and leave me, I'd make sure you see it matters, and you should come back."

"I told you—I'm staying. I'll find a way to continue with my business from here, and if I ever say a word about giving up, you remind me of this day and this moment. I'll stop and wait for you."

"If you run, you'll find me running with you, along with our houseful of children and all the dogs and cats."

"Houseful?" he asked, pushing his hand beneath the hair at her nape. "How many children?"

"How many bedrooms are there?" she asked, tracing the line of his jaw with kisses, reveling in her right to touch him. Her Jason. Her love. "I assume you put my office here because we're going to fill these rooms with sons and daughters?"

"We can do that," he said, looking slightly bewildered, instead of totally in charge. When she laughed, he stopped speaking to stare at her as if he needed to imprint her face on his mind. "When you sound so happy, you make me happy," he said. "I think hearing you laugh is what first made me want to believe the world was different than I'd known it to be."

"I should have laughed more often."

"You were perfect," he said, and lowered his head to brush her mouth with his. "Perfect for me, always. And I put your office right here because I knew you'd work best in the center of things. Because you're my center, Fleming, my reason to believe. You're the reason I believe I can live up to loving you the way you deserve, with all that I am."

She kissed him, and with her kiss, she offered him all her dreams. Because he embodied her dreams now. He'd become everything to her, family, friend, the love of her life, her future, and the only past she'd ever want.

"You are my Christmas gift," she said. "You are my happiness."

## *EPILOGUE*

ONE YEAR LATER, on Christmas morning, Fleming got up early and started her husband's train on the track beneath their Christmas tree. She plugged in the tree's lights and hurried to the kitchen to start coffee.

When she turned, Jason stood in the doorway, his hair rumpled, his cheek creased with lines from their pillowcases.

"Why'd you get up so early?" he asked.

"Because it's Christmas, and Santa left a little something for you."

He turned to the living room. "You always get your gift in first."

"'Always' meaning last Christmas and this?" she asked, pulling him toward the tree. She leaned down and picked up a box. "I had to wake you early because your grandparents will be up soon, and everyone else will arrive for breakfast, but I wanted you to be the first to know."

His grandmother and grandfather had spent the night upstairs in the new guest suite. Both sides of their family were joining them for their first holiday meal in the home they'd made together during the past year. Their memories had replaced any old ones that his mother or father might hold, and even they had promised to coexist through one meal per year.

Fleming had married the man she loved in front of the living room fireplace on Thanksgiving Day. He'd built a climbing tree for their new orange kitten, while the winter winds had gathered outside their newly glazed windows. Cooper, the kitten, was clinging even now to the top shelf of his own personal jungle gym while Fleming handed Jason a small box wrapped in Santas he'd never believed in before.

"Open it in a hurry," she said.

"It can't be another car for the train." He paused to distract her with a kiss that made her bones feel all warm and liquid. "Or another of my favorite cartoon characters."

"You'd know if you opened it." She glanced up the stairs. No one seemed to be stirring.

The sound of ripping paper brought her gaze back to Jason.

He pulled the top of the box off and then his breath caught as he looked inside. With one hand, he pulled out a tiny red T-shirt printed with white script: Daddy Loves Me Every Day.

The box hit the floor, but not before Jason drew Fleming close with so much tenderness she ached.

"Merry Christmas," she said.

"I love you. I love our family."

She lifted her face and willingly drowned in his eyes. "I love us, together. So much, Jason. Always."

* * * * *

# LARGER-PRINT BOOKS!
## GET 2 FREE LARGER-PRINT NOVELS PLUS
## 2 FREE GIFTS!

**♦HARLEQUIN**
*super romance*

## More Story...More Romance

**YES!** Please send me 2 FREE LARGER-PRINT Harlequin® Superromance® novels and my 2 FREE gifts (gifts are worth about $10). After receiving them, if I don't wish to receive any more books, I can return the shipping statement marked "cancel." If I don't cancel, I will receive 4 brand-new novels every month and be billed just $5.94 per book in the U.S. or $6.24 per book in Canada. That's a savings of at least 12% off the cover price! It's quite a bargain! Shipping and handling is just 50¢ per book in the U.S. and 75¢ per book in Canada.* I understand that accepting the 2 free books and gifts places me under no obligation to buy anything. I can always return a shipment and cancel at any time. Even if I never buy another book, the two free books and gifts are mine to keep forever.

132/332 HDN GHVC

Name _____ (PLEASE PRINT)

Address _____ Apt. #

City _____ State/Prov. _____ Zip/Postal Code

Signature (if under 18, a parent or guardian must sign)

### Mail to the **Reader Service:**
**IN U.S.A.:** P.O. Box 1867, Buffalo, NY 14240-1867
**IN CANADA:** P.O. Box 609, Fort Erie, Ontario  L2A 5X3

**Want to try two free books from another line?**
**Call 1-800-873-8635 today or visit www.ReaderService.com.**

\* Terms and prices subject to change without notice. Prices do not include applicable taxes. Sales tax applicable in N.Y. Canadian residents will be charged applicable taxes. Offer not valid in Quebec. This offer is limited to one order per household. Not valid for current subscribers to Harlequin Superromance Larger-Print books. All orders subject to credit approval. Credit or debit balances in a customer's account(s) may be offset by any other outstanding balance owed by or to the customer. Please allow 4 to 6 weeks for delivery. Offer available while quantities last.

**Your Privacy**—The Reader Service is committed to protecting your privacy. Our Privacy Policy is available online at www.ReaderService.com or upon request from the Reader Service.

We make a portion of our mailing list available to reputable third parties that offer products we believe may interest you. If you prefer that we not exchange your name with third parties, or if you wish to clarify or modify your communication preferences, please visit us at www.ReaderService.com/consumerschoice or write to us at Reader Service Preference Service, P.O. Box 9062, Buffalo, NY 14240-9062. Include your complete name and address.

HSRLP15